A NEW PACK FOR NEW YEAR

A KINCAID PACK PREQUEL

KIKI CLARK

A NEW PACK FOR NEW YEAR
A KINCAID PACK PREQUEL

❧

Injured and terrified, Victor runs for his life and right into the arms of the last person he expected to find: his true mate.

Living in a pack who viewed imperfections as weaknesses that needed to be eliminated, Victor is lucky to escape alive. He's heard of the Kincaid Pack's strong but fair alpha, but he has trouble truly believing he won't be targeted once more if his shameful secret is discovered.

When Cole meets a young man with fear in his eyes and pain in his scent, he recognizes him as his mate on sight. His excitement is short-lived, however, when they find out Victor's life is still in danger from what his old pack did to him.

After a lifetime of being abandoned by others, Victor has an important decision to make: Will he choose to trust the mate fate gave him?

Or will he run again?

A New Pack for New Year is a prequel to the best-selling Kincaid Pack series and features an eighteen-year-old wolf in need of some TLC, a thirty-something lion dying to give it to him, sexy times in an inappropriate place, found family feels, and hurt/comfort that will warm all the corners of your heart.

THE KINCAID PACK SERIES

A New Pack For New Year
(Cole & Victor)

The Alpha and His King
(Rick & Kai)

The Second and His Bonded
(Bennett & Kieran)

The Deputy and His Enforcer
(Marcus & Robson)

The Hunter and His Mates
(Gabriel & Jamie & Drake)

The Enforcer and His Heart
(Nico & Keegan)

The Witch and His Doctor
(Carter & Damien)

CHAPTER 1

*R*unning for his life was a stressful way to spend his eighteenth birthday, but Victor Rivera knew if he didn't leave his pack behind, he'd be dead by the next full moon.

He was lucky they'd failed to kill him during the last one.

Sprinting through the woods in his human form was slower than his wolf would have been, but then again, if he could easily shift into his wolf, he wouldn't be in the mess he was.

He didn't let himself focus on that at the moment though. The last thing he needed was to break down in tears of fear and frustration. At least he had his cousin Marcus he could run to for help. Though, he hadn't *seen* Marcus since his cousin was forced to leave their pack at sixteen and Victor was eleven.

Their pack really didn't handle *different* well.

The day Victor finally shifted for the first time, he'd never been more grateful he'd managed to keep in touch with Marcus. The look of horror on his parents' and alpha's faces was something he'd never forget. It had been bad enough that he was nearly eighteen before he had his first shift, when most in their pack had matured into their wolf by thirteen or fourteen, but barely being able to finish the shift even with his alpha's help?

His weakness brought shame on them all.

Marcus had been lucky in a way. Sure, his cousin had been treated horribly growing up and been banished from their pack as a teenager and forced to work for the Council for years. But at least he'd always been strong. His red hair, ghost white skin, and slender form had stuck out in their pack— marking him as different and thus *less than* the rest of them— practically since the moment of his birth.

His wolf had been big and strong though, and Marcus had shifted for the first time when he was *twelve*.

The fact that Marcus had joined a new pack a few years ago at the rank of beta didn't surprise Victor at all. Sure, Marcus was young and less physically imposing than a lot of betas and Enforcers, but Victor knew Alpha Kincaid must have seen what Victor's pack had failed to: Marcus's inherent value.

Leaving behind everything Victor knew was terrifying, but sticking around until his alpha tried to gut him again?

No thanks.

As he neared the place where he was supposed to find the car that had been hidden for him, he sucked in a breath to scent the air and grimaced, hand coming up to hold his ribs where the lingering pain was.

He really was lucky to be alive.

Before he could spiral further down into his memories of the last couple months, he caught the scent of a stranger and the distinctive odors of gasoline and motor oil. Sighing in relief, he darted forward, quickly finding the old, rusted sedan hidden under brush and branches.

When Marcus had offered to come and get Victor and Victor had declined—not wanting his new alpha to see him as weak and useless as his current one did—Marcus had still insisted on helping. He'd reassured Victor that another pack beta, Nico, had connections everywhere and could get him a reliable vehicle to make the journey.

As much as Victor had wanted to do everything on his own, he'd caved pretty quickly on the offer. Without any money, his only option had been to walk all the way to his new pack, hitch a ride with a stranger, or steal a car—none of which he'd been too eager to try.

He found the keys exactly where Marcus had said they would be in the center console. Firing up the engine, he didn't linger a second longer. He was technically outside his pack's territory already, but only by about a mile. Way too close for his comfort.

Shifting into gear, he gunned the car out of its hiding spot, taking the incline to the road easily, then sped north.

To his new pack.

Happy birthday to him.

When he was little, his mom used to tell him about how she'd been so sure he'd be her Christmas baby miracle. She and his dad had struggled for years to get pregnant, and just when she'd been ready to give up, she'd found out she was expecting. She would tell him about how happy they'd been and how they'd had the name Nicholas picked out and everything.

But when Christmas came and went, she'd realized he wouldn't arrive until he was good and ready. Just before the stroke of midnight on New Year's Eve, she'd finally given birth to her beautiful baby boy. The first baby to be born in their pack since his cousin Marcus, their alpha had called it a victory for the whole pack.

"That's when I realized you weren't Nicholas," his mom would say, smiling as she brushed her hand over the rounded

cheeks he'd had when he was young. *"You were Victor, our victory baby."*

As he crossed the border into Michigan, he wiped at a stray tear and tried to forget the disgust he'd seen on his mom's face the last time he'd seen her. Her sharp tongue ridiculing him and telling him she wished she'd never given birth to him.

That she would be glad when their alpha successfully killed him and ended their shame.

Having barely survived the last attack, he knew he wouldn't last another round with his alpha and that his parents wouldn't be helping him.

Which had only left running.

He was sure it would just be another instance in his parents' eyes of him being weak and a coward, but he tried not to think about that. Dwelling on his old life wouldn't help him start over in his new pack.

The farther north he drove, the heavier the snow fell until he had to slow down once he was past the state's capital, Lansing. The roads were getting slick, but he didn't want to stop. He'd found some cash in the cup holder and had been able to get gas, but there wasn't enough for him to stop somewhere for the night.

And what if his parents or alpha came after him?

He shuddered as he gripped the steering wheel until his fingers ached. He couldn't get caught outside of Alpha Kincaid's territory. There was a chance that they wouldn't bother trying to follow him, but he knew there was also a real chance that they would. That his fleeing and seeking shelter with another pack would be seen by them as bringing even more shame on their pack and want to drag him back.

To die at his alpha's hands.

A loud, shrill ringing sounded in the quiet car, startling him so badly he swerved. It took a second for him to correct, the slush on the side of the road trying to pull him off and into the ditch. He dug into the console once more and pulled out a cheap-looking phone.

"Hello?" he answered, knowing it had to be Marcus or the beta Nico, but his heart was still racing, fear tickling at the edges of his skin.

"Hello, Victor," his cousin's soft, formal voice greeted him, easing his fear. "I take it you made it to the car without incident?"

Victor smiled for the first time in... probably months. "Yeah. I was late leaving. My dad was watching something on TV and I had to wait for him to go to bed before I could sneak out."

Marcus made a soft sound, an agreement that he heard and understood. "I was growing concerned when you hadn't arrived yet. Are you having any difficulties with the weather? I could find you a hotel room to stop at for the night."

"I'm okay," he said, reveling in the fact that it was true for the first time since his debacle of a first shift. "I'm only about an hour from Meyerville."

He'd memorized the route and directions Marcus had sent him, knowing he'd have to leave his phone behind.

"If you're sure," Marcus said. "The warding at the edge of the territory will alert us when you cross it. Do you remember how to find the manor?"

"I remember."

"Alright. I'll see you in an hour then."

"Hey, Marcus?" he rushed out before his cousin could hang up.

"Yes?"

"Thank you. For everything."

There was a short pause, then Marcus murmured, "You're welcome, Victor."

He'd thought "manor" had just been some weird quirk Alpha Kincaid had where he insisted everyone call his house that.

The large, three-story... *mansion* was definitely a manor alright.

Luckily, he didn't have to stand in the freezing cold gawking for long. A familiar redheaded man opened the door right after he tentatively knocked. He'd have been impressed with the quick response if he hadn't had to input a code at the gate which had probably alerted everyone in the place to his arrival.

There was the tiniest quirk to the corner of Marcus's mouth as he ran his eyes over Victor's body in assessment. "Hello, Victor."

"Hey, cuz," Victor murmured, hesitating on the doorstep, then diving forward and wrapping Marcus in a hug. He ignored how stiff Marcus went and just breathed in the scent of family and safety for the first time in too long.

Finally, Marcus slowly raised his arms and very gently returned Victor's hug. They stood like that, both inhaling and savoring the moment, for several moments. Victor was content to stay tucked against his cousin's strong body, absorbing the feeling of safety, for the rest of the night at least. It was soothing the aching pain in his chest to be held so gently.

But a gruff voice behind Marcus forced them apart and into motion. "Damn, Marcus, we heating the outdoors?"

"My apologies, Alpha Kincaid," Marcus said, moving out of the way so Victor could step farther inside, then shutting the door firmly behind him.

Victor tried to brush the snowflakes off his clothes as fast as he could and ran a hand through his messy curls, knowing he still probably looked exactly like what he was: a poor, unwanted runaway. His jeans were clean, but so worn and thin they'd offered no protection from the cold and had holes in the knees from actual wear. His gray T-shirt was soft from too many washes and the red and black flannel he wore over it had frayed cuffs and was missing a button.

He tried not to feel embarrassed as he raised his eyes but kept his head tilted down out of respect. Marcus had stepped over and was standing just behind Alpha Garrick Kincaid, his silent presence a strange comfort to Victor.

Alpha Kincaid was... exactly as Victor had pictured him. Large and well-muscled, he had a bit of stubble on his firm jaw and a gaze that told Victor he'd accept zero bullshit. But there was also a small smile on his lips as he stepped forward and extended a hand.

"Alpha, this is my cousin, Victor," Marcus said, voice as formal as ever. "Victor, this is Alpha Garrick Kincaid."

"Rick, please," Alpha Kincaid said, giving Victor's hand a firm shake, then stepping back to give Victor space and crossing his impressive arms over his even more impressive chest. "I'm glad you made it alright, Victor."

The idea of addressing his new alpha so informally made Victor's skin crawl and a quick glance at his cousin got him a subtle head shake. Taking a deep breath—and ignoring the sharp pain that caused—he bowed his head and said, "Thank you, Alpha Kincaid. I am so grateful to you for allowing me to come here. I promise I'll stay out of trouble and not cause any problems for you. You won't even notice I'm here."

No one said anything for a moment, and Victor's low-grade apprehension began to spike. Had he already offended his new alpha somehow? Slowly, he peeked up at him to try and gauge how badly he'd messed up.

Alpha Kincaid was studying him, head tilted slightly to the side and nostrils flared as he carefully inhaled. There was a tiny furrow between Marcus's eyebrows as his eyes lingered on Victor's ribs, like he could tell something was wrong.

"Take a few weeks to settle in, then come see me again so I can make sure you're doing alright," Alpha Kincaid finally said, nodding decisively. "If you need anything before then, don't hesitate to ask your cousin or one of the other betas or Enforcers. I don't want you to fade into the background here," he added, gaze sharpening for a moment. "This is your home now, and I want you to be comfortable."

Victor nodded, unable to speak with the lump of emotions in his throat. Marcus had told him Alpha Kincaid was different, would welcome Victor into his pack without question, but to actually hear his new alpha tell him to ask if he needed something? It was so simple yet so different than what he was used to.

Alpha Kincaid nodded once more, then stepped forward and placed a big hand on the side of Victor's neck, moving slowly so he could step back if he wanted to. He didn't want to though. In fact, he closed his eyes and savored the warmth soaking into his body from that one point of contact, sucking Alpha Kincaid's scent into his lungs like it was a drug.

"Welcome to the pack, Victor," Alpha Kincaid murmured. When Victor's eyes fluttered open, he found his alpha smiling at him gently. "And happy birthday."

CHAPTER 2

"Momma! Where's the cheeseburger for table five?" Cole Browning called into the kitchen as he hurried by the pass-through window with a tray of drinks. *Momma's Diner* was about half-full, which was pretty good for lunchtime on New Year's Day.

When they'd opened the place four years ago, they would have been lucky to have a couple families eating in the diner at that time of day—holiday or not. Cole sent a silent thank-you to the goddess as he handed out drinks with a smile, grateful beyond description for Rick Kincaid. The town was actually starting to grow, though they were still a ways off from thriving.

When his mom had insisted on moving to the small town in Michigan with his little sister, he'd thought she was insane. She'd met Rick a few years before he'd become alpha when he'd passed through their old pack, staying for a week before moving on. Cole had kept telling her that she couldn't uproot Ericka's life on a whim, that she didn't really know Kincaid, but his mom had just smiled and told him that she did.

She had known the moment she met him that he was a good man and would make a good alpha. It wasn't until

Ericka, only sixteen at the time, had told him that she wanted to be a pack beta one day that he relented and agreed to come with them. They all knew she would never have been afforded the chance to be a beta under their old alpha, who'd been about as traditional as you could get.

Moving to Meyerville had been... interesting. Rick had only been alpha for about six months and the pack and town were on the brink of disappearing off the map. But his mom had insisted the pack and town would strengthen under such a strong alpha and opened the diner despite his arguments against it.

He'd never been so grateful to be wrong in his life.

The rest of their family—his other two siblings and their mates and children—had followed a couple of years ago, eager to be closer to their mom and join a strong pack that was continuing to grow. Having the whole family together had soothed his lion immensely, letting him worry less about them being separated and focus on the diner and getting Ericka graduated from high school and off to college.

He heard a ding as he headed back toward the counter, a new table's orders jotted down on his notepad. The cheeseburger that had needed to be refired for being "a little pink" was sitting on the ledge of the window.

"Thank you, Momma," he hollered, catching a tired smile from her before she went back to cooking. He attached the new slip on the order ticket wheel and snagged the plate.

After delivering the burger and apologizing again, he returned to the counter where someone was waiting to pay but their lunchtime server, Brady, popped up and took care of them.

Cole held his smile through the lunch service, running back and forth between tables and the kitchen pass for another hour, then slumped when there were only two pack-mates left in a booth by the front window. Brady was on his break—which always consisted of him on his phone in his car talking to his girlfriend.

"You all need anything?" he asked the two customers, not bothering to raise his voice.

They both waved him off, having only just gotten their food and started eating.

"Okay, I'll be in the back if you need me."

When he got to the kitchen, he saw Cynthia, the evening cook, had already arrived and was getting things prepped for the dinner crowd.

"Hey, Cyn," he said as he passed. She lifted her chin in acknowledgment but didn't stop what she was doing and neither did he. He and his mom needed to have some words. He pushed into the office and stopped in his tracks at the sight of her slumped over the desk, head buried in her hands. "Momma?"

Carefully scenting the air, he stepped fully inside the tiny room and shut the door behind him. He got notes of pain—which was normal for her after working a full shift on her feet nowadays—but overlaying that was anguish and fear.

"Momma," he whispered, kneeling on the floor next to her and laying a hand on her knee. "What's wrong?"

"You know what's wrong," she rasped, wiping at her face even though no tears had actually fallen. "I can't keep doing this. *Momma's* is done. I don't know why I thought I could open this place when I was so old."

"Don't say that. You aren't old and this place isn't going anywhere. Even if you aren't standing in that kitchen every day, this will always be your place. You hear me? We just need to find someone who's willing to learn from you." That had been the trickiest part about hiring Cynthia. Even though Cyn had experience in other kitchens, his mom had wanted to teach her the ways *she* did things. A lot of her recipes were handed down from her mother and were the cornerstone that *Momma's Diner* was built on.

"It won't be the same," she said, voice breaking.

"No, it won't. But it'll be better for you. How many times have I heard you say you want to spend more time with your grandbabies lately?"

She gave him a half-hearted smile. "That's true. They're growing up so fast and I feel like I'm missing it, spending all my time here."

"Exactly."

Sighing, she gave his stubbled cheek a soft pat. "Such a good boy. Who'd have thought that when it was all said and done, you'd be the only one of my babies interested in working with your poor momma?"

Not him. He was the oldest of four and had never taken any interest in his mom's dream of owning her own restaurant. He'd always thought if she'd really wanted to do it, she would have tried to open a place when she and Pops were younger.

But then Pops had died and she confessed to him a little while later that their old alpha had been preventing her from getting a loan for years. Because it "wasn't right" for a woman and mother to own her own business.

He'd offered to take a loan for her and she'd told him Pops had tried that a number of times, but with the alpha's brother running the only bank in town, they hadn't stood a chance.

"It makes sense though," he said, pushing to his feet. "I am the best of the four of us, and your favorite."

Her laughter as he headed back to the front was a soothing balm to his soul. Of course, he now needed to try and find a cook to replace her, which wouldn't be easy. He scowled around the dining room and turned to Cynthia, leaning through the pass.

"Still no word from Seth?"

She shook her head as she continued chopping.

Huffing, he added hiring a new busboy to his to-do list as

well. This was the third shift in two weeks the kid hadn't shown up for and that was two more chances than Cole normally would have given. But Seth was the son of one of his mom's best friends, so he'd been lenient with the kid.

Enough was enough though.

Pulling out his phone, he texted his sister Ericka.

Cole: *Hey, can you come help with dinner tonight? Seth no-showed again. Lunch was bad enough with just me and Brady.*

He tucked his phone back in his pocket, then went to check on the customers, making sure they didn't need refills or anything. The diner served breakfast, lunch, and dinner six days a week. Cole and Brady covered the dining room for lunch and dinner, his mom was in the kitchen for breakfast and lunch with Cynthia coming in for dinner, and then Ingrid —an ancient opossum shifter that had worked for the old owners as well—worked the front for breakfast. They weren't a big place, so the five of them plus a busboy to clear tables and wash dishes during rushes were plenty.

If everyone showed up.

His phone vibrated just as he was returning the change to his packmates in the booth and greeting a few new customers who'd walked in.

Ericka: *That little shit. Yeah, give me like half an hour and I'll be there.*

Sending a thumbs up emoji, he breathed a little sigh of relief. Ericka may not want to work at the diner full-time, but she had no problem busting her butt when she was there.

He was grateful that while she was home on winter break he'd been able to ask her to come in as often as he had. But she'd be headed back to campus in a week so he needed to hurry up and get them more help if he didn't want to run himself ragged when she was gone.

With that thought in mind, instead of tucking his phone away he double-checked that everyone in the dining room was taken care of, then dialed a number everyone in the pack had, but he'd never used before.

"Hello?"

The deep voice that answered sent a little shiver down Cole's spine. It wasn't fear, exactly, but even over the phone, he could hear the power in Enforcer Bennett Young's voice. As the pack's second-in-command, that made sense. In the five years Alpha Kincaid had been in charge, the pack had more than tripled in size. That many members gave the alpha and his inner circle of Enforcers a major boost in strength.

"Um, yes, hello. I'm sorry to bother you, Enforcer Young," Cole began, his neck prickling when the couple packmates in the diner heard him say the name and looked up at him.

"You're not bothering me." Somehow Young managed to sound soothing, his words calming Cole's rapid heart rate.

Clearing his throat, Cole said, "This is Cole Browning from—"

"*Momma's Diner*," he said, and Cole could hear the smile in his voice. "What can I help you with, Cole? Your mom okay?"

"Yes. Well… Yes, but she's part of why I'm calling. Let me step outside for a moment." He cast one more glance around, smiled reassuringly at the couple of worried eyes he caught, then slipped out the front door. The bitter cold stole his breath for a moment, but it was the only way to get any kind of privacy for the call. Luckily, he saw Brady stepping out of his car and hustling to the diner's back door, head down against the chilling breeze.

The diner sat on the corner of Main and Oak, but between the freezing temperature and the holiday, the streets of Meyerville were mostly quiet. He caught sight of one of the coven witches hustling into *Wicca We Can* across the street, but they didn't look up so he didn't bother waving.

"When we moved here," Cole started, already shivering, "you told us to come to you if we needed anything."

"And I meant that. What's going on?"

"As much as my mom loves the diner, working full shifts six days a week isn't something she can do for much longer. I need another cook, but I'm not sure where to start looking. Cyn just walked in one day and asked if we needed help, and the one busboy I hired needs to be fired." He stopped and took a deep breath. "Sorry, I just... I'm not sure if this is something you can even help with—"

"It is, son," Enforcer Young reassured him. He and Young were probably about the same age, but he wasn't offended by the *son* comment. Word in the pack was that Bennett Young took his job of taking care of the pack very seriously— everyone probably felt like a surrogate child to him. "With so many new members, helping folks find housing and employment is a big part of what we do."

"Thank you." Cole sagged back against the rough brick of the building. "That's... thank you. My family tries so hard not to be a bother, but I figured if nothing else, you could point me in the right direction."

There was silence on the other end, and Cole worried for half a second that he'd somehow offended the pack's second, but then Enforcer Young said gruffly, "You're not a bother. I'll be there in ten minutes, and we can talk more about what you need."

Cole barely had time to stutter out a thank you before Enforcer Young had hung up. He stood for a few moments just staring at his phone, his foggy breath filling the air around him, before he headed back inside. That had been easier than he'd thought. Even if Cole still had to interview a bunch of people, he knew they'd be packmates and not just any random person who happened to see their Help Wanted sign.

It wasn't that he was opposed to hiring humans, but there was a certain comfort in being surrounded by pack. Plus, that way he didn't have to worry about his family or one of the customers accidentally doing something suspicious.

Somehow, Ericka beat Enforcer Young to the diner, entering in a swirl of snow flurries and curly blonde hair. Her wide smile as she dusted flakes off her bright pink coat was infectious. Though is dropped from his face as soon as she sidled up to him at the counter and opened her mouth.

"So, are you worried about firing Seth after you guys..." She did some sort of horrifying hand motion that he assumed meant *had sex*.

Shooting her a glare, he looked around the diner for eaves-dropping packmates, but there were only three people in the place and they were all humans. Still. "What the hell?" he whispered harshly, turning his back on the dining area. "Seth and I didn't do *anything*."

"That's not what he said," she sing-songed, smile down-right evil. She pulled her wild hair up into a ponytail, never once looking away from his scowling face.

"I don't care what he said. Nothing happened." Though Seth had *wanted* something to happen. He'd tried to kiss Cole in the walk-in a couple weeks before and Cole had been hoping that his gentle rebuff would be the end of the awkward looks and flirting. And he'd sort of been right. Only instead, Seth had started no-showing for shifts.

"Hey, I was just teasing." She finally dropped her smirk and put a hand on his arm, obviously catching on to how upset Cole was getting. "He tried to tell me a few days ago that you'd been the one to come onto him, but I just laughed in his face."

But if he was saying it to Ericka, who else was he spreading rumors to?

He sighed. "Thanks. Will you go help—"

The door opened behind him, and even without looking, he could tell it was Enforcer Young. Not only did his lion immediately perk up at catching the scent that came in on the cold draft, but his sister's eyes just about popped out of her head. It was Cole's turn to smirk, but he wiped it from his face before turning to the entrance.

"Good afternoon, Enforcer Young," he said, stepping around the counter. "Thank you for coming. I really appreciate any help you can give me."

Cole was a big man, but his second-in-command? Young towered over him, his massive shoulders looking like they'd barely fit through the door. He was bundled up in a tan peacoat, thick scarf, gloves, and a knit hat, making him appear even larger and more intimidating, the power radiating off the tiger shifter. But the wide smile he gave Cole and Ericka as he tugged his hat and gloves off was warm, his dark brown eyes crinkling at the sides.

"You're welcome and call me Bennett," he said, tucking his things in his pockets then starting to unwind his scarf. "Or B. The formality makes me itchy."

Cole chuckled. "Got it. Are you hungry? I could grab you something before we get started—*oof.*" The sharp elbow Ericka delivered to his ribs knocked the wind out of him and drew Bennett's amused gaze. Scowling at his sister, he rolled his eyes at her significant look and turned back to Bennett. "Have you met my sister Ericka?"

Bennett laughed and stepped forward, hand extended. "Not since you all moved here. What was that? Four years ago now?"

"Four and a half, sir," Ericka gushed, taking Bennett's hand and shaking it hardily. "I'm twenty now."

"Okay," Bennett said slowly, eyeing Ericka then shooting Cole a questioning glance.

Cole didn't even bother interrupting, just leaned back against the counter and crossed his arms to wait until his sister finished her spiel.

"And I'm studying business at college. When you're finished with Cole, I hope you'll give me a few minutes of your time. I'd love to pick your brain about any particular classes you think I should take."

"That I think..." Bennett shot another confused look at Cole, but he just smiled reassuringly.

"Yes, sir. I'm going to be a pack beta one day soon, and I want to make sure I'm as prepared as I can be."

The smile that spread across Bennett's face was enormous. "A beta, huh? Well, I'll be sure to let Rick know."

CHAPTER 3

*V*ictor woke with a start, shooting upright in bed as his eyes darted around the unfamiliar room.

Just as Marcus's familiar scent filled his nose, his brain caught up to his surroundings and he remembered the night before. He'd done it. He'd actually done it! He'd fled his pack and family and made it to Rick Kincaid's pack and the safety of his cousin's home.

But what would happen now?

Before he could start worrying about fitting into his new pack or finding a job and place of his own—no way his stoically independent cousin would want him invading his space for longer than necessary—he heard footsteps approaching the closed door. There was a soft knock, then Marcus asked if he was okay.

Oh, right. There was someone around who'd actually care if his heart started to race and his scent soured with fear.

Clearing his throat, he said, "I'm fine."

Marcus hesitated on the other side, and Victor wondered what he'd do. Finally, he simply said, "Okay," and then walked away.

Flopping back onto the small bed shoved into the corner

of what was obviously Marcus's home office, Victor grunted at the shot of pain the movement caused in his ribs. He held a hand to his side and stared at the ceiling. For months, he'd been so scared all the time, and now even though he was free of his old pack, he was still afraid.

What was wrong with him?

Sighing, he shoved his covers off and carefully sat up once more. Lying in bed wondering what would happen to him wasn't going to make him feel better. He needed a plan and he needed to trust that Marcus would help him and not kick him out for staying too long in his house.

He dressed in one of the couple of outfits he'd thrown in his backpack and headed downstairs after stopping in the bathroom to relieve his bladder and brush his teeth.

Marcus was at his kitchen table, laptop open in front of him and focus completely on whatever he was working on. There was fresh coffee though, so Victor beelined for that, poured a cup, and carried it over, joining Marcus and waiting for him to finish what he was doing.

As soon as Victor sat, Marcus typed something and closed his computer, linking his hands together on top and studying Victor. "Did you sleep well?"

Victor nodded and sipped his coffee, trying to hide his grimace at the taste. "Yes, thank you."

"What's wrong with the coffee?"

He couldn't help but chuckle. "Nothing. I'm just not used to it."

Marcus narrowed his eyes just the tiniest bit but didn't call Victor on the lie.

"Can I ask you some questions?" He didn't want to talk about the terrible coffee; he wanted to figure out his next steps. The twisting in his stomach wouldn't stop until he had a plan in place—he knew from experience.

"Of course." Marcus straightened his shoulders, dropping

the subject and seeming to step into Beta Mode. "Anything you need."

He meant to ask where he could find a job, or see if Marcus would lend him a few more pairs of clothes, or maybe ask Marcus if he'd been as scared when he'd been forced out of their pack too.

But what came out of his mouth was, "Is Alpha Kincaid really better?" He slapped a hand over his mouth and stared at Marcus in horror. They'd already talked about this before he left, and Victor had been accepted into Rick's pack—why would he insult his cousin and new alpha by asking again?

"Yes," Marcus said, ignoring that Victor was freaking out. "I was nervous when I came here too, but Alpha Kincaid is a good man and a better alpha than most. I promise."

Victor sucked in a breath and let the words fill him up, calming his nerves and soaking into his battered soul. He knew it wasn't uncommon for alphas to be aggressive and brutish, but he also knew his old one was worse than that. That his old pack was suffering in a lot of ways, and almost all of them were because of the alpha.

"Thank you. I know you already told me that—"

"But sometimes we have to hear it again." Marcus nodded. "And sometimes hearing it isn't enough, but you'll see. I won't let anything bad happen to you here, Victor. You're safe now."

Tears filling his eyes, he looked away and swiped at them. "Thank you."

Marcus didn't respond, simply reached over and placed a warm hand on Victor's wrist and waited for him to compose himself. The gentle touch made it harder to stop the tears though.

They sat in the quiet kitchen for a long time as Victor silently cried and Marcus kept a grounding hand on him. It was almost like all the emotions Victor had forced himself to keep locked down for the last few months were leaking out of him now that he felt safe.

When he finally started to calm down, Marcus got up and came back with a box of tissues. It took Victor a few moments to get himself mopped up, and he was chuckling in embarrassment at the small mound of tissues he used.

"Wow, sorry about that."

"You don't need to apologize," Marcus reassured him quietly.

Victor smiled weakly but stopped before asking about a job when Marcus's green eyes darted away for a moment, the muscle next to his mouth flickering. "What's wrong?"

"Nothing is wrong," Marcus said slowly. "But I fear I may owe you an apology of my own."

"What? Why?"

There was a weighted pause, and Victor somehow knew before Marcus said anything what his cousin had done.

"You told Alpha Kincaid about my trouble shifting, didn't you?" Horror was seeping into his bones, turning him brittle once more, like the comfort he'd so recently felt was completely washed away. "But I… I asked you not to and you said…"

"I said," Marcus said carefully, holding Victor's eyes, "that I would only share with Alpha Kincaid what he needed to know regarding your transfer to the pack."

"And you said he didn't need to know about my shifting to accept it!" Victor shouted, pushing to his feet and striding away, rubbing at his upper arms to try and warm his chilled body. "You said he'd accept based solely on Alpha Hill's attempt to k-kill me!"

Goddess, Rick had to think he was so weak. A useless member of his pack who'd only been admitted because Marcus had been the one to petition for him. Marcus's strong wolf and sharp mind were of actual value to the pack.

Victor was just dead weight.

He'd so hoped no one would find out until he'd proven his worth in other ways.

Strong hands gripped his shoulders, halting his pacing and startling him. He couldn't meet his cousin's gaze, staring straight ahead at his pristine white button-up instead.

"And he did accept based on that," Marcus said, voice as even as ever but fingers biting into Victor's muscles. "But he needed to know you were struggling—"

"No, he didn't!"

"—so he could help you."

Victor's breath caught in the back of his throat, and he finally raised his eyes and studied Marcus's impassive face. "How could he help me? The healer said—"

It was Marcus's turn to interrupt, disdain clear in his tone. "That *healer* says whatever Alpha Hill tells him to. We have a real doctor and a strong coven. If something is wrong, I have faith we can fix it."

Victor narrowed his eyes. "If?"

Giving his shoulders one last squeeze, Marcus stepped back and leaned against the table, slipping his hands into the pockets of his slacks. "Yes. It's entirely possible—probable even—that Alpha Hill was the reason you could barely shift."

"How's that possible?"

"Why do you think there are so few children in his pack?"

The seemingly random change in subject rocked Victor back on his heels for a moment as he tried to figure out what Marcus was getting at. While Victor knew it was unusual for shifters to have fertility problems, he'd never really stopped to think why so many couples in his old pack had struggled for years or been unable to conceive at all. "I'm not... I don't know."

"A pack's strength—it's very health—begins and ends with its alpha. And Alpha Hill is weak in more ways than one."

Marcus's voice was so fierce, so sure, that Victor instinctively believed him.

"Think of a pack's magic as a tree," Marcus said, pulling

his hands free and placing them on the table behind him, seeming to relax into his role as teacher. "Every member of the pack makes up the branches, but the alpha is the roots. A tree can't grow without strong, healthy roots, and the bigger it gets, the stronger the root system becomes."

That made a certain sense to Victor. "So if the roots start off weak and unhealthy…"

"The tree will never grow. In fact, it can kill the tree if left untreated."

Victor stared at Marcus, eyes wide. "Metaphorically kill the tree or…?" He realized that a pack's inability to grow and thrive would be exactly like killing it. Eventually the pack would just… disappear. "Whoa."

Marcus just nodded and said, "With such a weak alpha helping you, I'm not surprised you struggled to shift. Would you mind telling me what you felt when he helped you?"

"What do you mean? I didn't feel anything."

Eyes widening just the tiniest bit, Marcus stared at him but then he nodded again. "That makes sense."

"Does it? All I know is that I couldn't do it on my own and my parents were…" *Furious.* "Anyway, they took me to the alpha's house, and he told me to try again. But he just, like, stood over me glaring as I struggled. It seemed to take forever, but I eventually did it. Except…"

Marcus cocked his head slightly. "What is it?"

Victor had to turn his face away from his cousin before he could answer, feeling the heat rise into his cheeks and embarrassment curl his shoulders inward. "I… I was so weak I could barely stand up."

Marcus made a noise like that also made sense to him for some reason.

Darting his eyes up to check Marcus's face for disgust and inhaling subtly, he couldn't understand why Marcus wasn't at least worried about Victor's weakness. "You don't think that's messed up?"

"I think how you were treated is... messed up," Marcus said, body still relaxed against the table. "And I think it's remarkable that you were able to force the shift without any help from your alpha. How long did it take?"

"Half an hour," Victor whispered, remembered shame making his voice raspier than normal.

Marcus shook his head. "I can't believe you were able to complete it."

"I didn't really feel like I had a choice if I wanted to leave the alpha's house in one piece."

The words hung in the air between them for several long moments, then Marcus cursed softly and pushed away from the table. Victor watched as he paced away, his anger like battery acid in Victor's nose.

It was kind of nice.

Victor knew that what had happened to him was horrible, but everyone in his old pack had acted like he'd deserved it. So it was almost a relief to have someone furious on his behalf for a change.

Marcus finally came back over and rested a hand on the side of Victor's neck, the same way Alpha Kincaid had the night before. Looking into Victor's eyes, he said softly, "I'm sorry I wasn't there to protect you, but I'll make sure no one ever hurts you again. I swear it."

He believed him, but, more importantly, his wolf stirred in his chest, rumbling in approval at the vow. Victor touched where he felt him, right between his pecs.

Marcus eyed the movement. "Can you feel your wolf?"

"Yeah. I felt something last night when Alpha Kincaid touched me, but I thought it was indigestion or wishful thinking or something. Except when I was trying to shift, I never really felt him before." Victor rubbed his chest, excitement building in his veins. His *and* his wolf's.

"Your wolf will continue to grow stronger now that you're part of a strong pack. In a few weeks, we can try your shift again with Alpha Kincaid. Though you may not need his help, I think it would be good for him to be present. In the meantime, we can have our doctor and one of the coven witches give you a quick look over just to be absolutely sure there aren't any underlying issues."

There was a thread of apprehension curling around his spine at the idea of failing to shift in front of his new alpha, but Victor pushed it away, deciding to trust that Marcus knew what he was talking about. "Okay, yeah. That sounds like a good idea."

Marcus's mouth twitched up into a tiny smile, like he knew how nervous Victor was, but all he did was give Victor's neck a reassuring squeeze and dipped his chin in agreement. "I'll be with you for everything."

As they separated, Victor felt excited about the future for the first time in a long time. "How do you know so much about this stuff?"

"My time with the Council was very educational." Marcus turned back to where he'd been sitting, settling back into his chair.

Victor studied him. His tone had been perfectly even, but there was a note of something in the air that he couldn't quite catch.

As he sat again too and listened to Marcus explain about different Kincaid Pack procedures, ceremonies, and customs, he tried to figure out what had happened with his cousin's scent when he'd talked about the Council. Victor's understanding had been that Marcus mostly acted as a personal assistant to one of the members…

That was it. The slightly sour scent had been longing. He realized Marcus must miss whoever he used to work for.

Victor wondered what it would be like to miss someone years after he'd left them. Without other kids his own age in the pack, he'd had very few friends growing up. Interactions with humans had been discouraged, leaving him without many options.

He realized with a start that he didn't even really miss his parents. Not the parents he'd known the last few years anyway as their anger over his lack of shifting had gotten worse and worse. The ones who would pretend he wasn't in the room or stare at him in icy silence when he dared to try and speak to them.

The ones who had stood by and watched with the rest of the pack as their alpha had stabbed him during the full moon celebration and declared him an abomination that would be sacrificed to the goddess.

If anything, he missed how his parents had treated him when he was young, when he was still their victory baby and not their bitter disappointment.

As scary as being part of a new pack was, he had faith in Marcus—and even a slowly growing belief in Alpha Kincaid —that things would be better in this one than his last.

Refocusing on the conversation, he pushed away his thoughts of the past and said a quick thanks to the goddess for helping him reach his cousin. Marcus may not have been the most demonstrative person, but Victor knew he'd make sure Victor had a roof over his head and food in his belly.

If a part of him wished for more, for someone to love and cherish him, then that was his secret to keep.

CHAPTER 4

*C*ole had to give Bennett his due—the man worked quick.

Four hours after their conversation at the diner, Cole had an email in his inbox with a list of ten candidates for a table busser/dishwasher. Six had experience in restaurants, three were under eighteen but came with personal recommendations from someone else in the pack, and the last had been included because they were brand new to the pack and related to a pack beta.

Cole wasn't sure he wanted to give someone a job just because of who their cousin was, but he'd be willing to interview the guy like the others.

Bennett had included email addresses for each of the candidates and told him to reach out to as many as he'd like. He'd also said to let him know if none of them were a good fit and he'd send another batch of names.

So far, the process was a hundred times easier than he'd been expecting. Even firing Seth had gone off without a hitch —though that probably had more to do with Cole not letting the guy get a word in edgewise when Cole called him after his missed shift and then hanging up. Seth had tried to call him back and sent a few texts, but Cole knew he'd lose interest and give up before long.

He'd emailed the six people with experience and the guy related to the pack beta, leaving the unexperienced teens for the second round if one of the others didn't work out. He'd much rather have someone who'd stick around than someone who left for college after a year.

Almost all of the people he'd contacted had responded that night, so he'd been able to set up interviews for the next morning before his shift. Hopefully, he'd know by the end of the day who his new hire would be.

Even the pack beta, Marcus Rivera, had responded, letting Cole know he appreciated his cousin being given an interview and he'd make sure to get Victor to the diner at the time Cole had given him. Cole was interested to see if Victor would do any talking or if his cousin would answer for him.

Cole thought he would lay awake all night worrying about the interviews and hoping Bennett had just as much luck putting together a short list for him regarding cooks, but before he knew it, his alarm was going off and it was time to get up.

As eager as he was to get the ball rolling with the interviews, he was going in earlier than normal and his groggy brain didn't like it. He'd never liked early mornings, which made his normal hours at the diner perfect.

When he strolled into the restaurant, eyes locked on the coffee station behind the counter, he inhaled automatically, expecting to take the intoxicating smell of the fresh brew directly into his lungs.

His feet stumbled to a halt.

There was something… delicious in the air. Almost like his mom's fresh-baked sourdough bread slathered with honey butter, but not quite.

He searched the dining room, head swiveling as he tried to pinpoint the source.

Where was it coming from?

"Morning," Ingrid said as she hustled past him, tray full of food. "You've got someone in the office waiting on ya."

She was gone before he could say anything or thank her for the info, already moving on to the booth in the front corner.

Glancing at his watch, he grunted in approval at his first candidate being early for their interview. He shook his head to try and dislodge the enticing scent as he poured a mug of coffee, nodded a hello to the packmates eating at the counter, then pushed into the kitchen and headed back to the office.

"Morning, Momma," he called as he passed her. She grinned at him as she flipped pancakes on the flattop.

"Morning, sweetie!"

He was glad to see she was in better spirits than she had been the day before. After meeting with Bennett and receiving his email, Cole had called his mom and let her know he was handling the hiring of more help and not to worry. He'd sort of expected some pushback since she was technically the boss, but she'd just sighed a little and agreed.

Stopping just outside the office door, he compulsively ran a hand over his buzzed hair and the stubble around his mouth, glancing down at his clothes to make sure nothing was amiss. They'd always been laidback on attire at the diner, but he'd put on his best pair of jeans and a dark purple button-up in an attempt to feel more like a supervisor.

The stiff collar was already making him feel suffocated and the thing wasn't even buttoned all the way up.

Just as he was turning the knob and pushing the door open, he realized the scent he'd caught as soon as he walked in was stronger outside the office. Eyes drifting shut, he took a huge lungful of the stuff into his body and held it.

Jesus, his cock was starting to stir in his pants. What the hell was happening?

"Um, hello?"

Lids flipping open, Cole pinned the young man sitting in front of the desk with his gaze, his lion rumbling to life in his chest. Inhaling, Cole didn't look away from honey brown eyes as he stepped inside and kicked the door shut behind him. He knew his eyes were probably glowing a little based on how the young guy's own widened in surprise.

Cole took in his messy waves, thick brows, and square jaw before running his gaze downward. Worn jeans with the beginning of a hole in one knee and a clean but too big black dress shirt began to paint a picture for him about the young man staring back at him.

Victor Rivera, cousin to beta Marcus Rivera.

And Cole's mate, apparently.

The man who walked into the office at *Momma's Diner* was enormous, but Victor wasn't scared. He couldn't help but suck in great draws of the man's intoxicating scent, ignoring the flashes of pain in his ribs, as the guy closed the door behind him and then leaned back against it. Glowing yellow eyes roved over Victor's face.

Was this how job interviews usually went?

The man had to be Cole Browning. Marcus had emailed him on Victor's behalf to set up the interview. The nice older woman in the restaurant's dining room had shown him back to the office and told him Cole would be with him shortly.

Cole was... overwhelming. It was hard to tell from where Victor sat, but he would guess the man was over six feet tall and his shoulders were nearly as wide as Alpha Kincaid's had been. But where the alpha's stern mouth and fierce eyes had been intimidating, Cole's wrinkled dress shirt and stubbled jaw made Victor want to cuddle up next to him.

Though his buzzcut and the sharp angle of his jaw gave

him a tough appearance that probably should have made Victor nervous.

Nervous was the last thing he felt as the scent of... Goddess, it was almost like the man smelled like the gardenias in his mom's garden.

Suddenly, Cole cleared his throat and looked away, his big chest heaving as he took a deep breath.

"Victor, I presume?" Even the man's voice was sexy, gravelly and deep and like a caress down Victor's spine. "Victor?"

"Hmm?" Oh shit, the man had asked him a question, hadn't he? "Oh, um, I mean, yes. I'm Victor." He pushed to his feet quickly and thrust out his hand. "Thank you for meeting with me."

Cole eyed his hand for a moment, then leaned around him to set his mug of coffee on the desk. Straightening, he met Victor's gaze again as his big hand engulfed Victor's smaller one.

"My pleasure," Cole murmured, not so much shaking Victor's hand as just holding it and running his thumb over the backside in a calming manner. Slowly, Cole drew his arm back but didn't release Victor, so he was towed in closer, until they were only a few inches apart.

He had to part his lips to try and get more air into his lungs, and Cole's dark blue eyes dropped down to his mouth and flashed yellow again. This close, Victor could get more notes of the man's scent—something spicy was underneath the light floral scent he'd first noticed, and it was making his body come alive.

Licking his bottom lip, Victor tried to catch a little of Cole's scent on his tongue, hoping to taste the enticing man. With a rough groan, Cole started to lean down, eyes still on Victor's mouth. Excitement shot through him, but also a thread of apprehension. What was happening?

"Is this part of the interview?" he whispered before Cole's mouth touched his own. They were so close he could feel

Cole's warm breath against his face. He tipped his head back automatically, offering himself to this man without thought. Their lips nearly touched, the heat of Cole's skin lighting off sparks of need.

"Funny," Cole murmured.

Before he could ask why that was funny, Cole closed the distance between their mouths, brushing his lips against Victor's so softly it drew a whimper from deep inside Victor's chest.

Cole growled in response, his free hand coming up to cup Victor's jaw. He carefully angled Victor a little to the side so their mouths fit together even better, more fully. As his eyes fluttered shut, Victor tentatively brought his unclaimed hand up to rest on Cole's waist. As soon as the contact was made though, Cole released a sort of broken noise, almost like he was in pain, and his palm slid to the back of Victor's head to hold him more firmly.

And then Cole took possession of Victor's mouth as easily as he held him in place.

Victor had never felt anything so amazing in his entire life.

After several long, drugging moments of their mouths moving against each other and tongues teasing at lips, Cole released his hold on Victor's right hand and slipped it around him, palming his lower back and pulling them closer together. Gasping, Victor grabbed at Cole's purple shirt, holding on for dear life as Cole slipped the tip of his tongue between Victor's parted lips and entered his mouth.

His whole lower half was throbbing and his knees had gone weak, but Victor held onto Cole for dear life. When he tentatively licked inside Cole's mouth, his wolf roared to life inside him, electricity racing down his spine and out to his fingertips.

Startled, he jerked back, clutching at his chest and staring up at Cole's heavy-lidded eyes.

"What's wrong?" Cole asked, running his hand up and down Victor's back soothingly.

"My wolf..." He wasn't sure how to explain it.

"He recognizes me, doesn't he? Just like my lion recognizes you."

Was that what had happened? Other than when he'd been trying to shift, he'd never felt his wolf react so strongly to something.

"How does he know you?"

Cole smiled softly, a tiny dimple appearing in his left cheek. Victor had the strangest urge to lick the small divot. "Our animals always know."

That didn't really clarify anything, did it? He wasn't sure if he should push for an answer or just step back and put the brakes on everything.

Cole frowned, his hold loosening a little. "Wait... Do you not know?"

Victor rubbed at his chest even though his wolf had gone quiet again. "Know what?"

"Victor, we're..." Swallowing loudly, Cole dropped his hands and looked away, a furrow appearing between his dark blonde brows. Not being touched anymore made Victor feel unmoored in a way he couldn't stand, like he was completely alone and adrift in the sea of new feelings.

"We're what? You're kind of scaring me," Victor said, his voice hushed as he tightened his grip in Cole's shirt. If Cole wanted him to let go, he'd have to ask because he couldn't make himself step back at that point.

Scrubbing at his face and leaning back against the closed door, creating even more space between them, Cole sighed. "We're mates, Victor. Or, at least, my lion thinks we are."

Oh.

CHAPTER 5

*C*ole didn't know what to do. At thirty-one, he'd thought a lot about how meeting his mate would happen, but the other person not even recognizing the mating pull? Never really occurred to him.

Victor stared at him in shock, his honey eyes had nearly been gold a moment ago when they'd been filled with heat and lust, but now they'd darkened once more. His sexy pink lips were parted and still damp from Cole's kisses. And even though he didn't remember running his fingers through it, his hair seemed even more wild.

Cole had let go and leaned back when he'd started to realize Victor didn't know why Cole had been all over him, feeling like a complete lecher and assuming Victor would want the space, but if anything, Victor was holding onto his shirt even tighter, his knuckles turning white. Was he too scared to move? Did he think Cole wouldn't be able to control himself in the enclosed space?

Eyeing his coffee on the desk, he wished he'd had more than a couple sips before setting it down.

"Listen, maybe we should—" He wasn't even sure where

he was going to go with that sentence, but luckily, Victor cut him off.

"How do you know that we're m-mates?"

He shrugged as he studied Victor's youthful face once more, his eyes narrowing as a horrible thought pierced his brain. "My lion recognized your scent," he murmured, then more forcefully, "How old are you?"

Victor's eyes widened farther at the harsh tone. "Eighteen. Why?"

"Jesus Christ." He rubbed at his tired eyes. His mate's growing unease and agitation was driving his lion crazy, driving Cole's instincts to sooth and protect, but he wasn't sure how to make the situation better.

"Is that bad?"

Victor's voice was so small Cole dropped his hand immediately, intent on reassuring his mate. "No, not bad. I just think your cousin might be pissed that the thirty-one-year-old supervisor you came in to interview with kissed you five seconds after meeting you."

It was Victor's turn to narrow his eyes. "If we're mates, then why does your age or job matter? Why would Marcus have an opinion about it at all?"

That *if* was like a punch to Cole's solar plexus, but he tried to hide his grimace. "It just looks shady as hell, okay? Especially since you don't... feel the same."

Blotchy redness appeared in Victor's cheeks, and he finally released his hold on Cole, stepping back a little and wrapping his arm around himself as his other hand continued to rub at his chest. "I'm sorry. Marcus says my wolf will get stronger now that I have a strong alpha though."

"Hey, wait." He snagged Victor's surprisingly firm bicep, stopping his retreat. "What do you mean? Was your wolf injured or something?"

He'd never heard of such a thing, but he supposed it was

possible. The idea that Victor had been hurt stole his breath, his lion snarling in outrage.

Victor ducked his head and shook it. "Not injured. Um, this is kind of hard to explain. And a little embarrassing."

"It's okay. Take your time." He led him back over to the chair he'd been in and waited until he was sitting before squeezing his arm and releasing his hold so he could go over and grab his own chair. He dragged it over and sat close enough that their knees touched. Holding out his hand, he was relieved when Victor didn't hesitate to take it.

Victor took a deep breath and winced, but Cole didn't get a chance to ask about it. "So what did Marcus tell you about me?"

"Not a lot. The email I got from Enforcer Young said you were new to the pack and Rivera's cousin. Then when I reached out to Rivera about an interview, he said he'd make sure you got here in time but that was it."

Nodding, Victor raked his free hand through his hair. Cole had to clench his own into a fist to stop himself from reaching out and offering more comfort. He knew how soft those loose curls were and wanted to run his own fingers through the disheveled locks more than anything. His fingers fucking *tingled* with want.

"Well, I got here a couple days ago. I, uh, had to leave my old pack for safety reasons."

Cole's nostrils flared, rage filling his veins so quickly he couldn't hold back his snarl this time.

Victor seemed surprised, but then a tiny smile tugged at his lips. "It's probably kind of messed up how much I like that you're mad on my behalf, huh?"

It was enough to puncture the balloon of anger growing in Cole's chest. Shoulders slumping, he freed his hand from Victor's hold and grabbed the front of the arms on the metal and plastic chair Victor was sitting on. He tugged him forward, wedging his knees between Victor's and getting them as close as they could get while still in separate seats.

"Not messed up," he murmured, finding both of Victor's hands and threading their fingers together. Victor's gasping hiccup soothed Cole's lion further. "I hope it makes you feel safe here though, knowing I'll never let anything bad happen to you again."

"You can't just promise that, Cole."

Flashing his teeth in a fierce smile, he squeezed Victor's fingers. "Just did. Now tell me more about what happened in your old pack."

Shaking his head but smiling softly, Victor continued. "Marcus says the alpha was weak so the pack was weak, and now that I have some distance from them, I can see what he means."

Cole nodded but didn't respond, waiting for the bit about Victor's wolf. He rubbed Victor's trembling fingers encouragingly.

"I can't..." Stopping, Victor turned away and cleared his throat. "My wolf has always been quiet. I can't... I'm only now starting to feel things from him, but Marcus said I'll feel him more as he gets stronger here."

Thoughts spinning, Cole nodded again as he studied Victor's profile. His thick brows were scrunched but his chin was raised almost defiantly as he stared at something across the office. A few pieces started to click together in Cole's head.

"Do you have problems shifting?" He asked it softly, gently, but Victor reacted like Cole had struck him, flinching away and dropping that proud chin to his chest.

No words were needed as the sour scent of shame and fear permeated the air. Unable to stop himself, Cole lifted a hand to caress Victor's face, but he froze when Victor flinched again. Emotions were swirling inside him like a vortex, but he reminded himself that Victor needed him calm, not raging, when he felt so vulnerable.

"Hey, look at me," he whispered, letting his hand fall back to Victor's lap slowly. Victor didn't turn his head, but his eyes peered up at him. "I bet your cousin is right and your wolf will get stronger under Alpha Kincaid."

Victor nodded as his shoulders loosened a little. "Me too," he said softly.

"But," Cole continued, wanting to make sure he was absolutely clear, "it won't matter to me if he doesn't. Or if you always have problems shifting."

Sucking in a breath, Victor finally turned to look at him head on. "You can't mean that."

This time, he let Victor see his hand coming, reaching over and gently running the back of his fingers down his smooth cheek. "The hell I can't. If I have to, I'll convince you the human way that we're meant to be together. I bet I could woo the shit out of you."

Gasping out a watery laugh, Victor turned into Cole's lingering touch, nuzzling into his palm. Cole grinned and started gently petting Victor, running his fingers through his hair and behind his ear. He watched, fascinated, as his mate's eyes drifted shut, a small smile on his lips.

His lion rumbled approvingly as the air cleared and the scent of sourdough bread came rushing back.

They never did finish their interview, but a half an hour later, Victor found himself sitting at the counter in the dining room, eating a plate of delicious blueberry pancakes. He listened carefully as Cole explained how the diner was run and what Victor's role would be. When a young smiling woman came in a little while later, he couldn't help but feel bad as Cole took her back into the office to let her know the position had already been filled.

He wondered if she actually had experience as he stared guiltily down at the last few bites of his breakfast. And how many others there were who'd been looking forward to their interviews only to be shut down before they had the chance to sell themselves.

"What's wrong, sweetie? The pancakes not sitting well with you?"

He shot his head up and stared at Cole's mom, unsure what to say. She'd eyed him curiously earlier when Cole had escorted him through the kitchen, but he hadn't paused to introduce them, saying he'd get to meet her after the breakfast crowd cleared out. Her light blonde hair was tightly curled where it had escaped her bun, and Victor wondered if that was why Cole kept his so short. She was smiling at him, but her eyes were sharp as they ran over him.

Did she know about him and Cole somehow? How would she feel when she did find out if she didn't know already? What if she thought he was too young too?

He ran a hand down his borrowed button-up, glad she couldn't see his worn jeans. What if she didn't think he was good enough to be her son's mate?

"No, ma'am," he finally said, choosing his words carefully. "They were delicious. I really liked the hint of lemon zest."

Her blue eyes—so like Cole's—widened as she looked from his face to his nearly empty plate. "Did Cole tell you I put lemon zest in them?"

"No, ma'am." Was she mad? He couldn't quite tell, and it was making him anxious. Inhaling, he struggled to find her scent under all the food smells layered over her.

"Hmm." She tapped at her lips thoughtfully, eyes going around the dining room. "You ever cook before?"

He sat up straighter, his spine tingling with awareness. Something was happening. "Only for myself, ma'am."

She waved a hand. "You can just call me Momma, sweetie. Everyone does. What kinds of things do you like to cook?"

Excitement began to bubble up in his stomach, and he had to squeeze his hands into fists under the counter to try and keep himself calm. "All kinds of things. I didn't have access to anything too exotic where I lived with my old pack, but I'll try just about anything once if I have a recipe."

Nodding, she didn't reply right away, seeming to be just taking his measure for a moment. "Okay," she finally said, "come on back into the kitchen with me."

She didn't wait for his response, just turning and pushing back through the swinging door. He floundered, looking around like someone would pop up and tell him what he should do, but no one was at the counter with him and Cole was still gone.

Take a deep breath, he straightened his shoulders. He could do this, whatever it was. He'd been basically taking care of himself for years as his parents had pulled further and further away emotionally. Their disappointment had been like acid dripping onto the back of his neck—painful and unpredictable. But he had the chance now to start over. His new pack had no expectations of him, and no one but his cousin, his alpha, and his mate knew about his difficulties.

Pushing to his feet, he stalled out as he realized he'd just referred to Cole as his mate. He couldn't stop the smile that spread across his face as he thought about the kiss they'd shared and wondered when they'd be able to do it again.

"You coming?" Momma was in the pass-through window, eyebrows raised in question.

"Yes, Momma." Her grin at his use of her preferred name widened his own smile.

As he hurried into the kitchen, hands trembling with eagerness, the morning server, Ingrid, came up to the pass with a new slip. Momma grinned and took it before Ingrid could attached it to the metal wheel.

"Alright, let's see what we can do together, okay?"

CHAPTER 6

*T*urned out, they could do a heck of a lot together.

By the time Cole and the woman came out of the office, Victor was getting the hang of the flattop and was mid turn on an order of pancakes. He had the bacon, sausage, and hash all going as well and was about to crack the eggs for the scramble when Cole was suddenly right behind him.

"What's happening here?" his deep voice rumbled in Victor's ear. It was nearly enough to distract him into dropping the empty shell.

"I'm stealing your new busboy, so hopefully you actually interviewed that girl that just left," Momma said from where she was putting the cold stuff together for the table's order.

There was silence behind him as he finished the eggs— they cooked so much faster on the flattop, he'd accidentally burned a couple of orders—but as he plated everything and slipped it onto the ledge in the pass, he heard Cole mutter something about how he had because he'd felt guilty.

"Momma says I'm a natural," Victor said proudly, turning to his mate with his spatula still in hand. He moved so quickly his borrowed apron twirled out around him like a debutante's dress.

Cole was smiling softly, arms crossed over his broad chest and sleeves rolled up to his elbows. Victor couldn't quite stop himself from running his eyes over the exposed skin, wondering when wrists and forearms had become so attractive to him. "Did she?"

"Yup." His grin faltered a little at Cole's lack of enthusiasm. "What's wrong? Did you change your mind about me working here?"

Cole's eyebrows shot up and his arms fell. "What? No, of course not. I just..." He shot his mom a look, color infusing his cheeks in an absolutely adorable way. Clearing his throat, he muttered, "I was looking forward to working with you out in the dining room."

Biting his bottom lip, Victor dropped his chin but kept his gaze on Cole. "Yeah?"

Huffing out a breath, Cole slipped closer and gently cupped the sides of Victor's face, tipping his head back up. Momma gasped behind him, but they both ignored her. "Yes. But if this makes you happier, then that makes me ecstatic."

Happiness lit up his whole body like he was a freaking Christmas tree. "Yeah?"

Chuckling, Cole nodded as he leaned down. "Yeah."

Victor was holding his breath, so eager for another kiss from his mate that he'd forgotten where they were until Momma cleared her throat.

"Um, as sweet as this is—kissing isn't allowed in the kitchen, boys."

With a grunt of frustration, Cole dipped down and pressed a quick, chaste peck to Victor's lips that still left him weak in the knees, then stepped back with his hands up in the air. "Fine. I guess I have to finish my interviews anyway. I've got one more coming today, then the rest tomorrow morning."

Catching sight of the clock on the wall, some of Victor's good mood evaporated. "And I have to get ready to go. Marcus will be here shortly."

After his not-interview interview, he'd texted his cousin to let him know he got the job and was going to eat breakfast while going over things. He was tempted to text him again and tell him to cancel the appointment because he was going to stay all day. But there was no way Marcus would agree after the pack doctor had squeezed Victor into his schedule.

Cole stopped at the dining room door and peered back at him. "If you want to stay, one of us could drop you off at his place later."

"I wish, but I have to go to Dr. Bell's office," he said without thinking.

Backtracking, Cole came right over to him once more. "What? Why? I thought you said you weren't injured."

Even Momma had stopped what she was doing and was focused on him, waiting for an explanation. *Way to make a good first impression*, he grumbled at himself.

"It's not for an injury," he said softly, dropping his eyes. "It's for... what we talked about in your office."

He chanced a glance at Cole and saw his frown, then Cole carefully raised one hand and put it directly over where Victor's ribs hurt when he wasn't careful. "I think I should go with you."

A part of him wanted that, wanted to have his new mate next to him all the time, but the rest of him worried that would be dangerous. He'd only had himself to rely on for so long, what would happen if he let himself lean on Cole only for Cole to leave if Victor's wolf *didn't* get stronger? As much as Victor wanted to believe Cole really wouldn't care, he couldn't help but see his parents' disgusted faces in his head.

"You don't have to do that," he whispered, wishing they were alone but also glad Momma was there as a sort of buffer, keeping the conversation from getting too deep. Of course, just as he thought that, Cole snagged his hand and towed him back toward the office. "Wait, I still have the spatula!"

"We have others," Cole said, not slowing down at all.

He heard Momma laughing but he was still scowling at Cole when he closed them into the office once more. Opening his mouth, he wasn't sure what exactly he was going to say, but Cole's mouth landing on his stopped him.

Moaning, he dropped the metal spatula so he could wrap both arms around his mate's shoulders and hold on tight. Cole's mouth was so firm under his soft lips, demanding entrance, his hands holding Victor's head and hip possessively.

After several long moments of their lips moving together, tongues touching and retreating in a drugging mimicry of what Victor hoped they'd be doing very soon, Cole finally raised his head, his big chest heaving.

"What was I saying?"

Victor shook his head and raised onto his toes, desperate for more of his mate's mouth. Cole gave him one more kiss, then jerked back.

"Your appointment. That's what we were talking about."

With a groan, Victor let himself collapse against Cole's chest. "Were we? I don't remember that."

Cole chuckled. "Well I do. And I'd like to go with you. Please."

The please sounded almost painful, making it obvious Cole wasn't used to having to ask nicely. Victor started laughing, not bothering to raise his head as he repositioned his arms so he more comfortably hugged his mate. As much as he'd loved the kissing, the comfort that was soaking into his body at the close contact was almost as nice.

When he didn't say anything, Cole palmed the back of his head and threaded his fingers into his hair, caressing him. "Can I go with you, Victor?"

"Sure," he murmured, snuggling in closer to all that heat radiating off his mate's big body. Cole was warming up parts of him he hadn't even realized were cold.

❧

Cole's lion felt settled in a way he never had before as he gently cradled his mate's body against him, just holding onto Victor's slight form and giving him as much time and comfort as possible. After a few minutes, Victor tipped his head back and rested his chin between Cole's pecs.

"I'll text Marcus that we'll meet him there," Victor murmured. The way he was staring up at Cole... Victor cocked his head. "Are you purring?"

"Hmm, yes. My lion and I are very happy."

Victor's sweet face slackened in surprise. "Because of me?"

Nodding, he gently ran his thumb over one of Victor's eyebrows and smiled. "Because of you."

Color suffused Victor's cheeks but he grinned widely. "I'm happy because of you too."

"Not just because Momma invited you into her kitchen? Not many people have had that privilege."

Victor laughed and pushed out of Cole's arms, pulling a cheap-looking phone out of his pocket and starting to type.

Cole leaned against the door, relaxed, and watched his mate, adoring the fierce concentration on his face as he carefully typed out his message. A moment after he sent the text, his phone beeped and Victor frowned.

"What's wrong?" He pushed off the door, ready to help in any way he could.

"Nothing really," Victor said, shrugging and shoving his phone back in his pocket. "Do you know someone named Tashmica?"

Cole nodded, snagging Victor's hands and tugging him closer. "Sure. Tash helps at the shop across the street sometimes. She's not the head of the coven, but I get the impression that's mostly witch politics."

"Witch politics?"

"Sure. She's great though. Why do you ask?"

"Marcus said she'd be at my appointment too."

Cole nodded and pressed a quick kiss to Victor's furrowed brow. "I'm sure it's just a precaution. Try not to worry until we actually know if there's something to worry about."

"Easier said than done," Victor scoffed, then sighed. "We should go though. I don't want to be late when Dr. Bell is squeezing me in."

"Okay." Cole didn't try to convince Victor he needed to relax. He had a feeling his mate wouldn't calm down until he knew for sure what—if anything—was wrong with his wolf. "Let's go."

"Do you need to reschedule your next interview first?"

"Oh yeah, probably. Just in case we aren't back in time." He gave Victor's fingers a squeeze before releasing his hands and stepping behind the desk. A few minutes later, he'd found a contact number for his next interviewee, called them, and rescheduled for the next day. He had to reassure them a couple of times that he wasn't blowing them off, but finally hung up with a little shake of his head.

"All set?" Victor murmured, looking at Cole with such tenderness it took his breath away.

Nodding, he came back around and snagged Victor's coat from where it was draped over the back of the chair he'd been sitting in earlier. Stepping close, he helped his mate slip into it, then grabbed his hand and kissed his palm.

"Let's go," he murmured and led him out. He lifted a hand in goodbye to his mom as they passed her. "I should be back long before the lunch rush, but Ericka will be here soon to help. And if Brady gets here before I get back, let him know I won't be long and he can reach me on my cell."

"No worries!" She grinned at him, the tiredness from yesterday seemingly forgotten as her eyes drifted to Victor and her smile turned soft. "You're welcome to come back afterward too, sweetie. Whatever you're comfortable with."

Cole glanced back at Victor and smirked at his blushing cheeks and ducked head. "We'll see how things go."

The grateful look Victor gave him for that simple answer made Cole's chest swell with pride. He'd do just about anything to keep Victor looking at him like that.

His own winter coat was hanging on a hook in the dining room where he always left it when he was working. He was just tugging it on when his sister stomped in, shaking snow off her boots and shoulders. When she spotted him, her frown was instantaneous.

"What the hell, Cole! I thought we were having breakfast and talking about..." Her voice trailed off as Cole grabbed Victor's hand once his coat was zipped up.

"I'll be back shortly. Victor and I have to run out for a bit." He had to bite the inside of his cheek to stop himself from laughing at her incredulous face.

"I'm sorry, what? Who the hell—"

"Ericka." His humor vanished as Victor took a step behind him at her loud voice.

Her quick eyes saw the movement too, her mouth dropping into a frown as she tugged her coat and hat off, hanging her stuff where Cole had just removed his own. "Sorry. It's nice to sort of meet you, Victor."

Victor stuck out a hand, smiling shyly. "Victor Rivera, new, um, line cook."

"Rivera?" Ericka turned wide eyes on Cole even as she automatically shook Victor's outstretched hand. She jerked her head back to Victor as the rest of what he'd said registered. "What do you mean new line cook?"

Laughing, Cole gently pushed past her, not releasing his hold on Victor. "Ask Momma. I was going to hire him to replace Seth but then she stole him out from under me."

She snickered, eyeing their clasped hands again. "You wish he was under—"

"Ericka!"

There were a couple of chuckles from other diners, but mostly people were used to the loud and sometimes inappropriate things that came out of her mouth. If Cole didn't love her so damn much, he'd be annoyed.

"Goodbye," he said firmly, pushing the door open.

"Bye, Ericka," Victor said, laughter in his voice.

"Later, Victor. Can't *wait* to get to know you better."

The diner's door swinging shut behind them couldn't completely muffle her cackles.

CHAPTER 7

"*D*o you know Dr. Bell?" Victor asked, not taking his eyes off the unassuming building they were parked in front of. It looked like it maybe used to be a house, but the sign in front clearly stated that Dr. Carter Bell, MD worked inside. Victor's old pack hadn't had a doctor and the healer had been... less than qualified. If you were injured badly enough, you were *maybe* taken to the human hospital.

Victor hadn't been that lucky.

He didn't realize he was holding a hand to his ribs until Cole's strong fingers wrapped around his wrist and squeezed. "It's going to be okay."

Tearing his eyes away, he stared at his... mate. Goddess, he didn't know if he'd get used to that word any time soon. "How do you know?"

"Because I do know Doc and he's a good man." Cole leaned over the center console and cupped the side of Victor's face with his other hand. "And your cousin and I will both be there the whole time. We'd never let anything bad happen to you."

Victor let his eyes flutter shut, his cool skin soaking up the warmth of Cole's touch. "And the witch?" he murmured, without opening his eyes.

"She's good people too. We'll be okay."

When he peeked a look at Cole, he wasn't surprised at the soft smile, and he couldn't help but return it. "Can I have another kiss for luck?"

Cole huffed out a laugh, his warm breath caressing Victor's lips just before he pressed their mouths together.

He'd never get tired of the way his mate tasted.

When Cole lifted his head a minute later, his pupils were dilated and cheeks flushed. It was a really good look for him.

"We should go in before Marcus comes and retrieves you."

Sighing, Victor nodded, though he took some comfort in how Cole seemed reluctant to release him, his fingers grazing down his face all the way to the point of his chin. Taking courage from Cole's calm face and demeanor, Victor sucked in a breath and pushed open his door.

He didn't feel the stinging winter wind or hear the crunch of snow beneath his feet as he slowly approached the clinic. He wasn't sure what made him more nervous: the idea of strangers poking and prodding at him or the chance that one of them could find something wrong. Something that would prevent him from ever really being connected to his wolf or shifting without struggling for ages.

Warm fingers slipped between his own and eased the tightness in his chest. Cole didn't waste time trying to reassure him with words, simply gave his hand a squeeze then gently tugged him forward from where he'd frozen halfway up the walkway.

There was a soft tinkle of a bell as Cole pushed open the door and entered a small waiting area, a reception desk directly in front of them. When the pretty woman behind the desk looked up, her smile was friendly but unassuming and somehow put Victor at ease.

"Can I help you?"

"They're with me." Marcus pushed open a swinging door to the side of the desk and gave Victor's and Cole's clasped hands an unreadable look. "Dr. Bell and Ms. Torres are waiting."

Victor ducked his head at the gentle reprimand. They might have been on time if he hadn't been unable to leave the car. Or asked for a kiss.

"Sorry," he murmured. He was glad when Cole didn't say anything, simply leading him past the reception desk, even though his scent said he was annoyed. Victor knew that Marcus didn't mean to make Victor feel bad—he just took things like punctuality very seriously. Especially since Dr. Bell was doing him a favor to see him on such short notice.

As they neared a cracked-open door, Victor was surprised when he caught Alpha Kincaid's scent just as a boisterous laugh rang out. He shot a look at Cole, who just smiled and mouthed, "Doc," before pulling Victor into the room behind Marcus.

It wasn't an exam room but a large office full of over-flowing bookshelves and an imposing desk covered in papers. Alpha Kincaid was sitting in front of the desk, chuckling softly and leaning forward with his forearms on his thighs. A large white man was behind the desk, slapping the top as he continued to laugh, and a gorgeous black woman stood off to the side, smiling indulgently.

Marcus moved to stand behind Alpha Kincaid, but Cole stopped them just inside the door and waited, the hold he had on Victor's hand being the only thing keeping him from bolting or freaking out.

Alpha Kincaid sat up and turned to smile slightly at Victor, his eyes giving Victor's and Cole's persons a non-sexual once-over. Victor was beginning to realize that was just a thing Alpha Kincaid did to make sure his pack was okay. He wondered if the alpha even realized he did it or if it was pure instinct to visually check them for injuries.

Dr. Bell finally settled down and grinned at them. "Victor, I presume?"

"Yes, sir."

"Rick was just telling me about how—"

Alpha Kincaid cleared his throat—not loudly or aggressively, just a soft sound that instantly stopped the words in Dr. Bell's mouth.

The doctor didn't seem upset, simply shrugging and leaning back in his chair. His dancing eyes dropped to where Victor clutched at Cole's hand, then settled on Cole's face. "How are you, Cole? Your momma doing okay?"

"She's fine, Doc. Getting tired of working such long hours, but Victor's going to help us out with that." Cole shot such a warm and adoring look at Victor, he felt his cheeks heat immediately, but he couldn't look away. Even when Dr. Bell started talking again, Victor had to drag his gaze back to the man.

"That's great. Victor, why don't you come sit down next to Rick, and Marcus, go grab another chair so Cole can keep holding his hand."

Alpha Kincaid stood. "Cole, you can sit here. I'm just crashing the appointment for moral support."

Moral support for Victor? He stared at his alpha in wonder, only moving forward when Cole gave him a nudge and Alpha Kincaid nodded toward the empty chairs.

Once they were settled across from Dr. Bell, the bear shifter leaned forward onto his desk and met Victor's eyes with a slight smile. "So. We all know why you're here, and I don't have time to beat around the bush. Tashmica will check your magic in a second, but I'm going to take a blood sample first."

"Okay," Victor said, shooting a look at the silent woman in the corner. Her bright red lipstick matched her dress perfectly, and her smile seemed genuine. Looking back at Dr. Bell, he carefully asked, "What sort of tests are you going to do? Will they... hurt?"

The surround sound of Cole, Marcus, and Alpha Kincaid all snarling or growling at once probably should have freaked him out, but Victor found it oddly soothing. Dr. Bell was already shaking his head as he grabbed a tray sitting off to the side, stood, and rolled his chair around his desk so he could sit next to Victor.

"No tests," Dr. Bell said, waiting as Cole helped Victor out of his winter coat and he rolled up his sleeve. "There's no point in putting you through a bunch of invasive tests at this time. I agree with Rick and Marcus that your magic will strengthen as a member of a strong pack. So unless Tashmica finds something in her exam, or you're still struggling in a month, we'll just do some basic bloodwork to make sure you aren't malnourished or anything."

"That makes sense," he said, finishing with his sleeve and slipping his hand back into Cole's waiting one. Extending his bare arm, he averted his eyes, not wanting to watch the process.

After a long minute of no one moving or saying anything, Cole finally leaned forward and brushed his lips across Victor's cheek in a barely there kiss and whispered, "He's waiting for you to give him permission."

"Oh!" Cheeks flushing, he jerked his head up and met Dr. Bell's amused eyes. "I'm sorry."

"That's okay. As a practitioner—and as a pack—we have very clear rules about consent. I should have made it clear that you can decline any part of today's or future appointments at any time, for any reason."

That was... Victor didn't even have words for it. He'd learned about consent in regards to sex in the public human school he'd attended, but no one had ever stated it so broadly as to include things like medical tests. As the silence stretched on without anyone getting annoyed or pushy, Victor felt his wolf stir in his chest.

Safe. He felt *safe*—truly and completely—for the first time since he was a child and thought his parents were infallible superheroes.

"I consent," he whispered, staring into the doctor's patient face.

Dr. Bell nodded once, then made quick work of drawing a few vials of blood. By the time he was done, the phone on his desk was ringing, and a few whirlwind moments later, Dr. Bell had disappeared with the vials, promising to return shortly.

The witch stepped forward after the door clicked shut, taking Dr. Bell's chair that was still next to Victor and setting a small bag on the floor at her feet. "Tashmica Torres," she said, extending her hand.

"Victor Rivera." He shook her hand, surprised at the strength in her grip. "This is—"

"Oh, I know Cole. I've eaten more than my fair share of Momma's blueberry pancakes."

"Haven't seen you in a while though," Cole said.

Tashmica rolled her eyes and flicked her fingers like they were damp. "Agnes."

"What's she on a rampage about now?" Alpha Kincaid asked from over by the window, a frown marring his brow.

"The order in which the grimoires are shelved," Tashmica said delicately, then huffed a sigh and shrugged. "I'm sure she's just trying to keep me busy for some reason, but hell if I know why."

The scent of his alpha's annoyance was a sting in his nose, but he didn't understand what they were talking about. He assumed Agnes was another witch and he thought grimoires were spell books, but he didn't know why she'd want to keep Tashmica busy or why that would annoy Alpha Kincaid.

Turning back to Victor, her red lips stretched into a slight smile. "Ready?"

Not sure what was going to happen, he nodded anyway. "Sure."

"I don't want you to be afraid," Tashmica said, tugging her bag into her lap and sticking a hand inside. "I'm going to take out a small knife and a bowl. I just need a couple of drops of your blood. You should barely even feel it."

"What do you need his blood for?" Cole asked, sounding almost angry.

"Our magic is in our blood. To make sure that his is okay, I need a little bit for a spell. Simple as that." She refocused on him, giving him an encouraging smile. "I'll just prick your finger. The spell only needs a couple of drops."

"It's okay, Cole," he whispered, leaning up and pressing a quick peck to his mate's cheek. He ignored the heat in his face as he turned back to Tashmica. "Do whatever you need to do. I want to know for certain everything is okay."

Her smile widened as she pulled a tiny dagger and stone bowl out of her bag. He extended the same arm Dr. Bell had drawn blood from and turned his head away, meeting Marcus's gaze from where his cousin stood across the room next to Alpha Kincaid. Marcus nodded once at him, reaffirming his willingness to step forward if need be.

A moment later, he felt a tiny prick, but the pain was minuscule and gone almost immediately.

Tashmica rolled the chair back so she was closer to Dr. Bell's desk and set the bowl on top. She pulled out a few tiny vials of herbs and started mixing things into the bowl, using another little stone piece to grind everything together.

No one in the room spoke as they waited.

Finally, Tashmica pulled out a small box of matches, lit one, and dropped it in the bowl. A plume of bright white smoke immediately rose from the bowl, the edges of which were tinted purple. It was almost beautiful in a way, but Victor wasn't sure what it meant.

"Is that... good?"

Tashmica was squinting at the smoke as if she was confused. Then she turned her narrowed eyes on him. "Victor, the white means your magic is fine, but the purple means there's wolfsbane present inside you."

Victor sucked in a breath, and Cole started growling next to him. He patted absently at his mate's arm, staying focused on Tashmica. "I, uh, was stabbed a little while back."

Marcus and Alpha Kincaid had already known about it, but even they were upset, his cousin demanding, "They stabbed you with wolfsbane?"

Victor cleared his throat and turned to face Marcus, wincing when he saw how pale Cole's face looked. "I was pretty sure the blade was laced with it. I got really sick and the fever that... consumed me while I was healing took a long time to break." He slowly raised a hand to his ribs. "Sometimes it still hurts."

Tashmica nodded like that made sense and ignored everyone else in the room, keeping her focus on Victor. "That's because it's still inside you. It's mingled with your magic. Can you show me where they stabbed you?"

Victor nodded and raised one side of his shirt. He didn't have to look to know that there was still a scar there. He assumed that was because of the wolfsbane. Tashmica rolled closer to look at the thin white line more carefully.

He wasn't sure what to make of the fact that Cole hadn't said anything. He knew he was upset, but shouldn't he be upset *for* Victor and not *at* him?

"Yes, from this angle it's likely the tip of the dagger nicked your ribs. That would've transferred the wolfsbane from the blade to the bone, and from there, it'll work into your bone marrow and then spread throughout your body, sort of like an infection or cancer. Does it hurt anywhere else in your body?"

He shook his head quickly. "No, no. Just here and just if I strain, get worked up, or breathe too hard."

"Oh, only then," Cole muttered, rubbing his thumb over the back of Victor's hand, obviously wanting him to know he wasn't trying to make Victor feel bad. The small touch helped calm the crawling anxiety working its way up his spine.

Tashmica reached over and patted his wrist, nodding. "That's good."

"How is that good?" Alpha Kincaid growled, stalking closer and coming to stand right behind Victor, placing his hands on the back of his chair as a blatant show of support and protectiveness.

"Because that means it hasn't spread throughout his body, and we should be able to remove it much easier."

"What would've happened..." Cole cleared his throat, his voice husky with emotion. "What would've happened if you hadn't found the wolfsbane?"

Tashmica didn't look away from Victor, holding his gaze without flinching. Victor didn't need her to say it. None of them did.

But with a steady voice, she answered, "He would've died."

CHAPTER 8

*C*ole wasn't sure why he had to have her say it. It wasn't like he didn't know that was what the answer was, but a part of him needed it said out loud. Not just for himself, but for the whole room. Because he knew Victor probably wouldn't have said anything about the pain in his ribs on his own. And if he'd noticed Victor was in pain, Cole was sure Marcus and Alpha Kincaid had too.

And sure, he'd planned on bringing it up if none of the others did, but what if Doc hadn't come back before they'd left? Would he have remembered to follow up before the poison had spread to other parts of Victor's body? Would they have been able remove all of it if it'd gotten to, say, his heart?

What if they hadn't? What if his mate had died right after Cole had found him?

The thought was almost too much to bear, his chest tightening and his breaths turning shallow. He couldn't hear what was being said over the buzzing in his ears; couldn't feel Victor's hand in his own, only the sweat accumulating on his temples and under his arms.

And then a strong hand was gripping his shoulder,

bringing him back from the brink and anchoring him to the moment.

He glanced up and over his shoulder at his alpha, his rock in that moment. Alpha Kincaid's eyes were full of compassion, but there was a little bit of fear there too.

He knew that Rick was wondering the same thing he was: what if they had all missed it?

"I'd like to wait for Doc to be finished in the other room," Tashmica was saying, her tone brisk but not unkind. "We can do it right now in an examination room. I'm sure Doc wouldn't mind giving you a local anesthetic, so you won't feel a thing."

Victor shot him a nervous look, and Cole tried to smile reassuringly. He asked Tashmica, "What would you have to do to get it out?"

"Well." Tashmica shot a glance at Cole, then refocused on Victor. "It sounds a lot scarier than it is, okay? What we'll do is have Doc create a small incision right along your current scar, and then I'll use magic to draw the wolfsbane out."

Victor didn't respond for a moment, but his fingers tightened a little where they were still entwined with Cole's. He heard him swallow thickly.

"Okay. Let's do it."

It didn't take long for Doc to rejoin them in his office and then Cole followed the three of them into an exam room. There wasn't enough room for everyone, but Victor said he wanted Cole there. There was a light scent of hurt from Marcus, but he didn't show it. Instead, he and Rick agreed to wait in the office. It helped that Tashmica said it would only take a few minutes once they were started.

When Victor removed his shirt and climbed up onto the table, Cole forced himself to shrug off his lingering doubts and fears and focus on giving comfort to his mate. He stood on the opposite side of where Doc and Tashmica would need to work, grabbing Victor's hand and pressing their palms together, sinking the fingers of his other hand into Victor's soft curls.

"Keep your eyes on me," he rumbled, locking gazes with Victor. He could practically see the whites of his eyes he was so scared. "I'm right here. No one's going to hurt you. I'm right here."

Victor sucked in a breath and let it out slowly. The scent of fear and anxiety slowly lessened in the room. "I believe you," he whispered back.

Cole didn't look away from Victor's face, keeping their eyes locked. A few minutes later, Tashmica said softly, "We're ready."

Victor didn't look away either. "Do it."

There was movement out of the corner of his eye, but it wasn't until his lion caught the scent of his mate's blood in the air that things became real. Victor flinched at one point, just as Tashmica's chanting grew stronger, and it was all Cole could do to stop himself from turning and roaring at Doc and Tashmica.

He caught the sickly-sweet scent of wolfsbane about a minute later, and his gut clenched painfully.

Right after that, Doc said, "We're done. You did really well, Victor."

He watched as Victor sucked in another breath, that time expanding his lungs as far as he could, and then smiling up at Cole. "It doesn't hurt anymore."

"That's good," he murmured, leaning down and pressing a gentle kiss to Victor's smiling mouth. "I'm glad it doesn't hurt anymore."

Tashmica and Doc slipped out of the room quietly, giving them a moment to themselves. Victor sat up and Cole wrapped his arms around him, hugging him tightly and letting himself feel for a moment the sheer terror of almost losing his mate. Victor held on just as tightly, obviously knowing how close they'd come to losing each other too.

Eventually, they pulled apart just enough that Cole could pepper kisses across his face and jaw, down to the side of his neck. He couldn't resist placing a delicate kiss to the spot where he hoped one day his mating bite would be.

"We should get back in there," Victor said, his voice reluctant. "When we're done, can I go back to the diner with you?"

"Absolutely. Anything you want."

When they re-entered the office, Tashmica stopped what she was saying about an upcoming pack celebration and turned to smile at them. "Your cousin said that the wolfsbane poisoning happened after you had trouble shifting. Is that right?"

Victor nodded. "Yeah, my alpha wasn't happy about how shitty I was at shifting. He was surprised that I lived, probably thinking the wolfsbane would kill me even though the stab itself wouldn't have."

"I'm sure he did." Tashmica stood, hooking her bag over her shoulder and smiling at him and Victor. "Now that the wolfsbane is out of your system, you and your wolf will grow stronger. In a couple of weeks, I think you should try shifting again under Rick's guidance. If your wolf doesn't get stronger on his own, there are some herbs we can use to jumpstart the process. But I don't think it's necessary to speed things up since you aren't sick or in danger. Give yourself and your magic time to heal and you should be just fine."

Victor swallowed nervously but nodded. "Okay, thank you for everything."

She smiled, patted Victor gently on the cheek, and then slipped from the room quietly.

"If anything turns up in your bloodwork—which I don't expect it to—I'll give you a call and we can go from there. But otherwise, yeah, I agree. Give yourself some time to grow strong and then let Rick help you shift. Don't try and do it on your own though, and don't rush it," Doc said from behind his desk. He was leaning back casually and shot a look at Rick and Marcus standing by the window. "I'll give you guys the room for a minute."

As he moved past Victor and Cole, Victor thanked him too, and Doc gave him a nod and a quiet, "You're welcome."

Cole was watching Rick and Marcus though. Rick was looking at Marcus in a way that Cole couldn't interpret, but Marcus was staring at the ground.

Sighing, Rick clapped a hand on the side of Marcus's neck and stepped forward. "Victor, I want you to know that you're safe here and that we will always protect you."

Victor stiffened next to him. "I know that."

Cole narrowed his eyes. "What happened?"

Rick turned to Marcus. "You should tell him. Keeping him in the dark doesn't protect him. We do."

Cole and Victor exchanged glances and then focused on Marcus. "Tell me what?" Victor asked.

Marcus exhaled, and Cole figured that, for him, that was as good as a gusty sigh from someone else. He raised his head and met Victor's gaze head-on. "It wasn't that I wanted to keep you in the dark, per se. I just felt it was unnecessary to share information that would do nothing except terrify you."

Victor grabbed at Cole's hand blindly. "He wants me back, doesn't he?"

When Marcus's mouth opened but no words were forthcoming, Rick stepped forward, giving Marcus's neck a squeeze then dropping his hand.

"Your old alpha sent a message yesterday that if we were to see you, we were to return you to him."

"So he doesn't know Victor's here?" Cole asked, frowning.

Victor and Marcus both shook their heads, but it was Victor who answered. "No, I destroyed my cell phone before I came here, and Marcus and I only spoke over the phone, not through text. So if my parents looked at the bill or contacted the company, the best they could do was see that I was talking to him, not what I was saying."

"So he knows that you're here, but without proof couldn't just demand that Alpha Kincaid send you back."

"Exactly," Rick said, crossing his arms over his chest and widening his stance slightly. Cole was a big guy, but standing before his alpha always made him feel like a cub: small but safe. "He's weak and he knows it. So not only will he not demand anything of me, but he also won't risk coming here or sending someone here to get you. From the message, I almost got the impression that he was reaching out as more of a formality or because he was being pressured to by your parents, not because he actually wanted you returned." Rick quirked a half grin at them. "No offense, but I don't think you're worth it to him to go to war with me."

Victor huffed a laugh despite the situation, and Cole's affection for him grew. "No, I can't imagine I am. Especially since he tried to kill me anyway. If anything, he'd want me back just to finish the job."

Rick strode forward and clasped a hand to the side of Victor's neck, his other one coming up to mirror the move on Cole's. "But just in case, that's why we had you wait until you turned eighteen. He has no standing to demand your return. As an adult, you're allowed to request a transfer of packs any time you please—that's shifter law. You came here with permission and were welcomed into the pack, so it's done." He leaned forward, pressing his forehead to Victor's. "No take backs."

"No take backs," Victor whispered back.

Love and admiration for his alpha filled Cole's chest. Some days, it was hard for his lion living in a place with so many months of winter, but when he got to see Rick Kincaid in action, Cole knew that moving was the best decision his family could've ever made.

Rick gave them both a squeeze and then quietly excused himself, leaving Cole and Victor in the room with Marcus. Cole didn't really know the man well, but what he did know was that Marcus may have been young, but he'd come into the pack as a beta. And there were already rumors that he was going to be made into an Enforcer soon.

As Victor walked over and started quietly talking to his cousin, Cole studied him. While Marcus wasn't as big and broad as most Enforcers tended to be, there was a strength in his stoicism, something that let you know he could be trusted. That he could shoulder any burden thrust upon him.

After Victor told Marcus he wasn't going home with him but was going to return to the diner with Cole, Marcus met Cole's gaze and seemed to take his measure for the first time since he'd entered the room. Cole couldn't help standing a little straighter and throwing back his shoulders a bit. He knew that Marcus had to be worried because Victor was young, but he hoped that Marcus would see that Cole would never hurt him. That he would learn to know that truth in his bones. That Cole would always protect Victor.

No matter what.

Finally, Marcus nodded once, gave Victor's bicep a squeeze, and then strolled toward the door. He only paused for a moment to shake Cole's hand and then he was gone. No words were exchanged, but Cole knew he had at least passed the first test.

Turning to his mate, he couldn't help but smile at the worried look on Victor's face. "What's wrong?"

"'What's wrong'? Seriously? You and my cousin just had, like, the longest stare down ever. I wasn't sure if you were going to start fighting or kissing."

That made Cole laugh really hard, the idea of kissing anyone else literally causing him to bend over and slap at his thigh. When he finally caught his breath and could stand back up, he found Victor glaring at him playfully.

"That was not that funny," Victor said with a small pout.

The sight of his lower lip sticking out distracted Cole from the conversation, his lion rumbling to life as he stalked forward.

"Cole." His name left Victor's mouth on a sigh, a single breath filled with want.

"You shouldn't tease me with that lip," he said, his voice barely more than a rumble.

"Your lion's eyes are beautiful," Victor whispered, staring into Cole's face with wonder.

Rhythmic purring filled the space between them, and Cole wrapped his arms around his mate, pulling him close. "Let's get out of here."

"Back to the diner?"

"If that's still what you want."

Victor's smile made him so damn gorgeous. "That's totally what I want."

CHAPTER 9

"Is this your place?" Victor asked as they drove down a rutted, dirt driveway toward a dilapidated two-story house. They'd driven outside of town, but Cole had turned off the main road after only about ten minutes. The back road they'd been on for a while had had a few houses scattered every few hundred yards, and Cole had pointed at each one and told Victor who lived there.

They were all packmates. The idea of being surrounded by pack even outside the city limits made Victor breathe easier, especially after the news he'd gotten the other day about his old alpha contacting Alpha Kincaid.

The last few days had been the best of Victor's life though. He spent hours and hours at the diner with Cole and his mom and sister, learning about the business and Momma's recipes. She'd even let him experiment the day before with a few things he'd found online, grinning when she'd tasted the turkey, bacon, and avocado panini.

When he wasn't with the Brownings, he was spending time with Marcus, trying to connect with him on a deeper level before he left. Even though he and Cole hadn't talked about moving in together and were taking things slowly—

ridiculously slow in Victor's opinion—he knew it would happen sooner than later. Before he wasn't under the same roof as his cousin, he wanted to make sure their relationship was as strong as it could be. Marcus wasn't the easiest person to get to know but he'd started to open up more, sharing stories with Victor about working for the Council and some of things he'd seen since joining the pack.

One night, Nico—the beta with connections everywhere apparently—had stopped by Marcus's house to introduce himself. Victor had been glad he'd gotten the chance to thank him for the car that he'd driven to safety, but seeing how he'd teased Marcus had eased the worried part of Victor. He'd been concerned about leaving his cousin alone in his quiet house again, but he'd realized when he was watching the two of them together that Marcus was slowly building a life in the pack too.

Victor's good mood over the last few days hadn't even been spoiled when the old busboy, Seth, had come into the diner to pick up his final check and tried to imply he'd been in a relationship with Cole. It had been so obvious he was just upset about being fired and was trying to make Victor jealous. And the possessive way Cole had kissed him after Victor had laughed in Seth's face?

He shivered just remembering it.

"I don't live here, but I own it, yeah," Cole said, drawing Victor out of his thoughts as he slowed to a stop near the lopsided porch attached to the house and put the Jeep into Park. He made no move to turn the vehicle off or get out though. "I bought this place about a year ago. I guess I had this fanciful idea that I could fix it up and then have a place of my own, away from my mom and sister."

Victor stared at the house, seeing more and more problems the longer he looked. "Um. That's very ambitious of you."

Cole laughed heartily, slipping a hand over Victor's thigh and giving it a squeeze. "That's one word for it. I liked how close it was to the woods"—he nodded to the tree line not far from the back of the house—"and it was quiet out here, separate from the noise of town or lots of people like the apartment complex a lot of single pack members live in."

"I guess I can see how that might appeal to someone," Victor said carefully, wondering how he could tell his mate that the idea of being so isolated from everything sounded horrible to him. Even though things in town were slow because of the cold weather, Victor was loving how easy it was to walk to different shops and he'd been working hard to get to know other members of the pack as they came into the diner. He felt... alive and *connected* in a way he never had in his old pack.

Leaning over the center console, Cole was chuckling again when he pressed a reassuring kiss to Victor's cheek. "Don't worry. I'm not going to ask you to live out here."

He slumped in his seat in relief. "Oh thank god. I think I'd go crazy out here without anything to do."

"You act like it'd be an hour drive to town," Cole grumbled half-heartedly.

"Felt like it," Victor teased back, feeling safe to do so now that he wasn't worried about hurting Cole's feelings.

"Hardy-har-har."

"So what are you going to do with it?"

Cole turned to the building, his brows lowered in thought. "Not sure. The plot of land is actually a decent size, so it probably wouldn't be too hard to unload it, but I'm not sure..."

"What?"

He shrugged and turned back to Victor. "I'm not sure I can sell it to just anyone, even if they are pack. Is that okay?"

Victor frowned and sat up straight once more. "Why wouldn't I be okay with that?"

Running a hand over his short hair, Cole winced at him. "The property taxes on the land aren't cheap. I... I brought you here because I wanted you to know this is probably the dumbest, most impulsive thing I've ever done. And it'll affect us as mates. Once we're living together, we won't be able to afford a place of our own while we still have this—"

Victor cut off his rambling with a hard kiss, gentling things once Cole's mouth softened under his own. What had started as a way to distract his silly mate from worrying about silly things quickly turned into something very *not* silly.

Cole took control, his tongue taking possession of Victor's mouth in a way that was becoming achingly familiar. As much time as they'd spent together the last few days, stealing kisses in the diner's office or making out in Cole's Jeep when he dropped him back off at Marcus's was as far as things had gone, and it was starting to drive Victor crazy. He wanted his mate fiercely, but he was beginning to realize he'd have to be the one to take things a step farther. Cole was still a little worried about Victor's age, like in five or ten years he'd regret meeting his mate at eighteen.

As far as Victor was concerned, he was the luckiest shifter in the world. He was going to get to spend nearly his entire life with his mate, and that wasn't something a lot of their kind could say.

When he realized he was contemplating the merits of climbing over the center console or dragging Cole into the backseat, he pulled back, panting harshly against Cole's damp lips so they could finish their conversation. "I don't care where we live," he murmured, unable to resist giving a quick nibble to Cole's bottom lip. "And if this is the dumbest thing you've ever done, I think we'll be okay."

"What if it takes me ten years to find the right person to sell this place to? I can't explain it, but it feels like I need to... save it for someone special. Like I was never meant to live here, just hold onto it until the real occupants arrived." Cole thumped his head back against his seat and groaned. "Fuck, that sounds really corny."

"Maybe, but I think it's sweet too. I'd never ask you to do something that made you uncomfortable," he added, staring into his mate's worried eyes. He slid his hand up from where he'd used it to brace himself on Cole's chest, rubbing his thumb against the frown tugging at the corner of his mouth. "And I love the idea of living with your family. It'll give me years to laugh with Ericka, and learn to cook from Momma, and practice making love to you quietly."

Cole sucked in a breath, his body tensing as his eyes flared yellow. "Careful there," he growled.

Victor just smiled as he pulled his hand away and sank slowly onto his own seat once more, pressing his back against the door behind him so he was facing his mate. "What's wrong?" he asked quietly, trying his best to sound innocent, but based on Cole's flared nostrils, he was pretty sure his scent was giving away his game. "Don't you want Ericka and I to be friends? Or is it all the cooking I'll be doing with Momma that has you worried?"

A rumbling purr filled the enclosed space, sending shivers down Victor's spine as he slowly unzipped his coat. Cole's eyes seemed to glow even brighter as he watched Victor's fingers move down his body, then pull the sides of his coat apart.

"What are you doing, mate?" Cole's voice sounded deeper, fuller, like his lion was just beneath the surface, and it made Victor's balls throb as his dick began to harden behind his jeans.

Victor chuckled softly as he started on the buttons of his shirt, his fingers trembling just a tiny bit. He was trying to look sexy and confident, but without any experience in seducing someone, he wasn't sure how he was doing. "Just... getting more comfortable."

He wasn't sure Cole even heard his answer, his focus seemingly transfixed on the skin Victor was revealing down his chest. The scent of gardenias and spices filled the small space they were in, soaking into every pore of Victor's body and taking up all the space in his lungs.

Victor thought he could live off the scent of his mate's arousal for the rest of his life and die happy.

When Victor pushed his shirt out of the way, hands scrambling with his growing desire and impatience, Cole finally tore his eyes away, scanning outside the vehicle then eyeing the backseat with a frown. "Victor, I don't know what you're planning, but there's no way we'd both fit back there."

"I know," he said, laughing and unbuttoning his jeans. When he started on his zipper, Cole's glowing eyes landed on him again in an instant. "I thought..." He had to stop and clear his throat, his nerves nearly getting the best of him. Inhaling, he used the scent of Cole's desire to reassure him that his mate wouldn't laugh or think he was being ridiculous. Over the last few days, he'd felt his mate's eyes on him almost constantly, watching him as he did the most mundane of tasks. Whenever he'd caught Cole staring, he'd always found heat in his blue eyes and hunger on his face. "I thought you could watch me... touch myself. You like watching me, don't you?"

Cole sucked in a breath, his big chest expanding as he dragged his eyes up Victor's body to meet his gaze. "I didn't bring you out here for—"

"I know," he interrupted, pausing with his jeans still mostly covering his erection and leaning forward. Clasping the sides of Cole's face, he pressed a sweet kiss to his mouth that was quickly turned into something more, Cole's fingers digging into his skin and his tongue into his mouth. Victor let his mate take everything he wanted from the kiss, giving everything of himself.

Victor moaned as Cole threaded his fingers into his hair and shifted Victor's head so he could kiss him a little deeper. Even though he was losing control of what he'd started out wanting to do, Victor couldn't find it in himself to care. The feeling of Cole's tongue thrusting into his mouth, running over his teeth and palette and tangling with Victor's own, was driving him crazy in the best way possible.

Cole's other hand slipped around his back under his coat and shirt, caressing down his spine and dipping into the back of Victor's jeans, palming one buttcheek over his underwear. Victor ripped his mouth away to gasp as he arched into the touch.

"Cole," he murmured, voice raspy with need. "You keep touching me and there won't be a show to watch anymore."

Cole chuckled, squeezing the cheek he held. Victor hissed at the feeling of Cole's fingers digging into his crease, pressing his underwear against his sensitive skin. "Well, I wouldn't want to miss out on seeing your sexy show."

When Cole slipped his hand out of Victor's pants, he collapsed with a groan against his chest. Victor sucked in a few breaths, trying to regain his equilibrium. Finally, he pushed himself back so he could see Cole's smiling face.

"You know what's weird," he murmured, leaning back in to rub his nose against Cole's.

"What?"

"I feel like I've known you for ages, but really it's been less than a week. Isn't that weird?"

When Cole didn't respond right away, Victor scooted back so he could see him better and was surprised to see him frowning.

"If you don't want to do this anymore," Cole started, his words slow and careful, "we don't have to. We have the rest of our lives to be together and explore everything we like."

Victor bit his lip and resettled on his seat, back braced on the door. "I like when your eyes are on me, Cole. Can we explore that now?"

Releasing a ragged breath, Cole nodded loosely, hand shifting down to squeeze where Victor could just make out a hard line behind his zipper. "Yeah, yeah we can do that."

He focused on pushing his pants off and pressing his lips together so he didn't giggle at how on-board Cole sounded with Victor's plan. He knew it was probably a little strange that this would be the first act of intimacy between them, but he didn't really care. Every night since they'd met, he'd lain in the small bed in Marcus's office and jerked off thinking about Cole's eyes on him, remembering how his gaze had felt on his body all day.

Victor wasn't quite ready to exchange bites, not while there was still that kernel of uncertainty in him about his wolf, but he wanted to move them in that direction. Their connection as mates had been so strong from the moment they'd met, even with Victor's instincts being weakened. And Cole had been amazing from that very first moment. He hadn't gotten angry when Victor hadn't realized right away that they were mates, and he'd dropped everything to go with him to Dr. Bell's office, holding his hand the entire time. Then he'd welcomed him into his family's business and been patient with him as Victor had begun to learn what it meant to not only be a member of the Kincaid Pack, but a part of Cole's family.

And now he'd driven Victor out to see the place Cole considered his greatest failure because he wanted Victor to know it would affect their mating.

The day the goddess assigned mates, Victor had won the lottery, and he planned on giving her thanks every day for the rest of his life.

Tossing his jeans into the backseat, Victor laughed at the expansive feeling of joy and anticipation filling his chest. Cole raised his brows, but he was smiling still, watching Victor's every move like the feline predator he was.

His breath caught at the idea of his mate stalking and claiming him, the image crystalizing in his mind so clearly it was practically a premonition.

"What was that thought?" Cole murmured, running his

eyes over Victor's exposed legs and reaching over to turn the heat up a little.

"I'll tell you later," he said, smiling softly at the gesture even though they were both probably going to be sweating by the time they were done.

He started pulling off his coat and shirt, suddenly overcome with the need to show his body to his mate, to present himself. A firm grip on his arm stopped his movements.

"It's too cold," Cole said, shaking his head.

Victor laughed. "I feel like I'm burning up every time you look at me."

Cole swallowed, staring into Victor's eyes as his own lit back up, his lion obviously okay with the idea of Victor getting naked. Finally, he just released his hold and leaned back, pulling his own coat off and tossing it in the back with Victor's clothes.

When Victor leaned back to wiggle out of his underwear, the glass of the window was freezing against his shoulder blades, but he ignored it, focusing instead on the heat pooling in his belly.

Rather than throwing the briefs in the back with the rest, he grinned and tossed them at Cole's face, but of course, his mate caught them before they landed. His grin melted into a moan as Cole pressed them to his nose and inhaled, his purring filling the space once more, practically rattling the windows. When he started rubbing them on his cheek, covering himself with Victor's scent, Victor couldn't help but gasp and grab at his aching erection.

His whole focus became his mate's glowing eyes and the feeling of his fist slowing working his dick. To tease himself was to tease his mate, and he was discovering he *really* enjoyed that.

Usually when he jerked off, he did it fast, as a way to relieve himself and little else, but under Cole's unyielding gaze, he found himself taking his time and doing his best to draw it out.

When he slipped his other hand down to squeeze his testicles, Cole licked his lips. When he pulled his foreskin up over his head and hissed, Cole moaned and leaned forward a little. When he couldn't take the slow pace any longer and started stroking himself faster and faster, his mate grunted and snuck a hand down to his own dick.

"D-don't," Victor gritted out, his back arching as he felt his orgasm building at the base of his spine. "Wanna make you come."

"Jesus, Victor. Watching you is going to make me come."

He shook his head, eyes squeezed shut, and whimpered as he focused just under the head. He couldn't force the words out, but he hoped Cole waited for him. He wanted to taste his mate more than anything.

The sound of a zipper lowering had his eyes flying open and locking on the sight of the large bulge in Cole's underwear visible in the open V of his jeans. When Cole tucked his thumbs under the waistband of his gray boxer briefs and tugged, lowering the elastic band until it was tucked under his heavy looking balls, Victor was riveted at the sight of his mate's hard cock and yelled out his name as he started to come.

He kept moving his hand, working every last drop of semen out of his aching balls as he licked his lips and eyed Cole's long, thick erection straining up toward his belly button. The vein running down the underside was prominent, the head glossy with precome, and Victor had barely stopped coming when he was falling on it, mouth open and tongue extended.

CHAPTER 10

"Fucking hell!'" Cole barked out the curse as Victor damn near choked himself on his cock.

His hips bucked up involuntarily at the sudden warm, wet heat wrapped around the top half of his dick, firm tongue sweeping around his head. He groaned as he realized Victor was licking the precome off him like a damn lollipop, his hand fisting in his mate's messy curls and slowing his eager movements. "Easy, darling. You're about to make me pop off like a champagne bottle."

Victor whimpered, fighting his hold, so damn ready to try and swallow Cole's entire cock. The scent of his mate's come in the air and the curved line of his spine leading to his pert ass sticking up in the air were enough that his concern for trying to slow things down melted away. His lion was roaring in triumph as he loosened his hold and leaned back, wedging himself between his seat and door.

Moaning, Victor bobbed his head, his technique non-existent but his enthusiasm more than making up for the occasional scrape of teeth. When he felt Victor's tongue wiggling into his slit, he growled and regripped his soft hair. Victor's muscles practically liquified as he let Cole take over moving his head up and down.

"That's it," he murmured, letting his eyes fall shut for a second. Victor could only really go about halfway down, but it was enough that he had Cole right on the edge. "Tighten your lips a little more, oh fuck yeah. So good."

Victor seemed to soak up every little piece of encouragement or direction like a sponge. Before long, he was working the rest of Cole's cock with his hand and focusing his mouth on the head, just how Cole liked, and Cole was pretty sure he was going to die. That his mate was about to kill him with his first damn blowjob.

"Little faster," he murmured, flexing his hips just a bit as Victor sped up both his hand and his mouth, rubbing his tongue on the underside of Cole's head on every upstroke. "Mmhmm. Fuck, you're so good at this. I changed my mind," he panted out, switching the hand in Victor's hair for his other one—which was really so he could prevent his eager mate from gagging himself too much at that point than give actual guidance—so he could run his fingers down Victor's smooth back. He stopped just above the crack of his ass, his horny little mate arching and pushing his round backside higher in the air. "You can't work at the diner. We're both quitting in fact and staying locked up in my house for the next month. You probably won't be able to walk by the time we're done."

Victor made a sort of gurgling snorting sound that Cole took to mean he thought Cole was joking. Which he was... mostly. A not small part of him thought the idea held a lot of merit though.

He refocused, tightening his grip slightly in Victor's hair as his orgasm strained to release, his shaft throbbing in time with his rapid heartbeat. Slowly, he slid his middle finger down the crease of Victor's ass, petting the furled muscle of his hole with the pad when he reached it. Victor moaned as he tried to keep up his pace and spread his legs as far as they could go on the Jeep's seat.

"So gorgeous," Cole murmured, pressing just a little harder on Victor's opening, but backing off as soon as Victor slowed his movements on Cole's cock. He chuckled at the disgruntled sound his mate made before sealing his lips around the head of Cole's dick and sucking. Hard. "Fuck!"

There was no stopping his release. As much as he wanted to draw out the moment, their first time together, he couldn't stop his balls from drawing up and forcefully ejecting his come down his cock and into his mate's waiting mouth.

"Holy shit." He could barely catch his breath, stars still sparking behind his eyelids, when Victor pulled off his dick with an obscene slurp.

"That was great," Victor rasped, his voice so gravelly Cole could barely understand him.

"Fuck, I don't have any water in here," he said, twisting around like a case would magically appear in the back of his Jeep.

"It's okay," Victor croaked, pulling himself upright, then climbing over the center console. Cole cursed and tried to help him, but the space really wasn't big enough for both of them. Victor had to settle for sitting sideways on Cole's lap, his torso turned so he could bury his face in his throat, because Cole just took up too much room for him to straddle his legs.

He carefully wrapped his arms around his mate, noticing how delicate and slender he seemed now that the haze of lust wasn't clouding his eyes. Tipping his head back against the headrest, he palmed the scar on Victor's ribs and tightened his other arm when Victor shuddered against him.

"Cold?"

Victor shook his head and pressed closer, one arm worming around to grip at Cole's back and his other hand coming up to press Cole's more firmly against the permanent mark on his mate's skin. They sat like that for a long time, the heavy scent of their arousal still thick in the enclosed space. Cole took comfort in his mate's slight weight and smooth skin as his mind couldn't help but return to the dark place it had gone to in Doc's office a few days ago. He'd done well pushing the thoughts aside as he'd spent time getting to know his mate and watching him already begin to blossom under a strong and caring pack, but the knowledge of how close they'd come to losing Victor was never far from his mind.

"Don't think about it," Victor murmured, pressing a kiss to the thin skin of Cole's throat.

He huffed. "I can't stop thinking about it. About how I almost didn't get to have this." He had to stop to clear the emotion out of his throat. "I'm so fucking lucky that you're so strong."

Victor scoffed. "I'm not strong. I was terrified for years, worried I'd never be able to shift, that something was wrong with me. Then scared when I could finally do it, but only just barely. And knowing that my parents were okay with our alpha killing me?"

The sour scent of Victor's fear was nearly enough to over-power the smell of desire and come lingering in the air. Wrapping his arms more firmly around his mate, he offered as much comfort as he could, rubbing at Victor's exposed skin and murmuring soft words about how safe he was now.

When the scent eased, Cole continued their conversation. "Scared or not, you got yourself out of that place. You survived. Fuck, Victor, you were strong enough to survive wolfsbane poisoning. Not everyone can say that."

Victor pressed closer. "Turns out I had something pretty important to live for."

Cole frowned at the deflection but let the subject drop and held him as close as he could, figuring Victor just wasn't in a place where he could see himself clearly. Luckily, Cole had...

oh, at least fifty years to convince him. The thought made him smile as he stared out the windshield over his mate's head. For once, the sight of the crumbling house didn't fill him with regret or anger.

No, as the cold, dreary winter sun filtered through the overcast sky, Cole couldn't feel anything but hopeful about the future. About spending the rest of his life keeping Victor safe and watching him grow in confidence under the unconditional love his family would show his mate.

About claiming his mate and falling in love.

The day may have been gray and miserable, but Cole felt like he was sitting in a patch of summer sunshine.

He and Victor stayed out at his property for quite a while, whispering dreams about the future and sharing tidbits of their pasts. When his phone rang for the third time as the sun was setting, Cole had finally dug it out and answered. His sister had told him there was an issue with the inventory and he needed to get to the diner right away. He was annoyed that the others couldn't handle the problem without him. They were closed on Mondays, handling inventory and prep and he'd usually get caught up on invoices, but he'd taken the day off to spend with Victor.

Which she damn well knew. She also knew it was the first Monday he'd taken off since the diner had opened.

Victor was still straightening his clothes by the time Cole rolled into town, turning toward Main Street. He eyed his disheveled mate and grinned. "You may want to do something about your hair..."

Eyes wide, Victor whipped down the sun visor to inspect himself, then turned a scowl on Cole. "There isn't anything wrong with my hair, you jerk."

"Jerk?" Cole slapped a hand to his chest, right over his heart. "You wound me, mate."

He turned into *Momma's* parking lot—which seemed fuller than it should have been, but sometimes people used the lot for other businesses when they were closed—and slipped into his usual spot right at the end.

When Victor didn't respond, he turned a raised brow on him as he shut off his Jeep. Victor had a tender look on his face that stole Cole's breath. "What's that look for?" he whispered, leaning over the console to steal a kiss.

"I like when you call me mate," he murmured against Cole's lips.

"Oh yeah?" Cold pressed one more kiss to Victor's mouth. "What about—" He growled as he leaned back and dug out his ringing phone, rolling his eyes when he saw it was his sister again. "What, Ericka?"

"Stop canoodling in the parking lot! I need help." She hung up before he could respond.

Victor was snickering behind his hand, warm brown eyes dancing with amusement. "I guess we should go inside."

Muttering under his breath about interfering sisters and unsympathetic mates, Cole stepped out into the cold twilight, scowled at the few flakes brave enough to fall on him, and met Victor at the front of his Jeep. He didn't pause as he clasped their hands together and strode determinedly toward the front of the diner, Victor scrambling to keep up and giggling. It was hard for Cole to hold onto his frown as the infectious sound rang out in the still air.

"Luckily she's moving back into her dorm at the end of the week," Cole said, just to hear Victor laugh again. As annoying as his baby sister could be, he'd actually miss her though. She brought such energy into every room she was in and her determination was admirable.

But he wouldn't miss the interruptions to his *canoodling*.

Victor started to say something as they turned around the

corner of the building, but they both drew up short at the sight of all the people they could see inside the diner through the large front windows.

"What's going on?" Victor's voice was quiet, his hand tightening on Cole's.

"Not sure," he murmured, pulling his mate the rest of the way to the door and into the diner. The small crowd quieted at his entrance, most everyone turning to smile at them and his sister moving to the front with a shit-eating grin. "What's going on?"

"Surprise!"

He and Victor exchanged looks, then turned back to her in confusion. When he spotted his mom hustling forward, laughing, he moved toward her. "Momma, what did you two do?"

"We just wanted to have a little party to welcome Victor into the pack and celebrate his birthday and your mating." Her smile was wide and full of happiness, but Cole couldn't help but blush.

"Momma, we haven't, uh…" Dear god, he didn't want to tell his mom—especially in front of a crowd!—that he and Victor hadn't *actually* mated yet.

Victor elbowed him out of the way and wrapped his mom in a hug. "Thank you so much, Momma. This was incredibly kind of you. No one's celebrated my birthday in years."

"Oh sweetie, when you say things like that I just want to bundle you in a hundred blankets and force you to drink gallons of hot cocoa." Her eyes were sad as she met Cole's over Victor's shoulder, but his mate just laughed.

"I love hot cocoa."

A throat cleared off to the side and Cole realized other people were waiting to speak to him and Victor, the first being Alpha Kincaid.

"How are you settling in, Victor?" Kincaid asked, sipping

his mug of coffee as he nodded at someone across the room who called his name.

Victor stepped away from Cole's mom and ran his hands over his hair again, like he was suddenly worried their alpha would know what they'd been up to just by looking at him. Cole wasn't sure if he should remind his mate or not that Rick could *smell* what they'd been up to—along with everyone else in the room.

"Really well, alpha," Victor said, lips twitching into a nervous smile. Cole knew he still struggled with accepting the easy affection Alpha Kincaid gave to his pack members, but he was proud of his mate for trying. "Cole and his family have been really good to me, and Marcus... Well, I'm not sure if I'd still be alive if it weren't for him."

Cole looked around and saw Victor's cousin standing with a few other pack betas and Enforcers, nodding at something Enforcer Wilkins was saying. He appeared so serious even among those who were close friends, but Victor had told him about how horribly Marcus had been treated by his parents and their old alpha because of how he looked. It didn't make sense to Cole, treating anyone different as a punching bag, but he knew it wasn't completely unheard of. The Council basically allowed packs to be run however the alpha liked as long as they didn't break shifter laws in the process.

Alpha Kincaid clapped him on the shoulder, dragging his attention back to him and Victor, and Cole smiled apologetically. "Sorry, alpha."

Kincaid waved him off. "I just wanted to make sure you heard me say congratulations on your mating. I can't stay but I wanted you both to know how proud I am of you."

As their alpha moved over to the group of betas and Enforcers, Cole knew his mate wasn't the only one damn near glowing from Alpha Kincaid's praise. He turned to his mom when she sighed dramatically behind him.

"I'd like to point out that I never said 'I told you so' about him, but I was clearly right," Momma said, giving him a wink when he groaned and tipped his head back. "Well I was."

Victor had gotten dragged away by Ericka and was being introduced to the rest of their siblings and their mates. Cole couldn't look away from his mate as Victor accepted Cole's youngest niece into his arms. He stared at her with such yearning he knew he'd have to find a way to give Victor a cub of his own one day. Or a pup. Cole wasn't picky.

"That young man is very special," his mom murmured, giving his wrist a squeeze.

As Victor threw his head back and laughed, Cole's heart squeezed so hard it hurt, but it was the best kind of pain. The kind he wanted to experience for the rest of his life.

"He really is, Momma. I'm so damn lucky."

CHAPTER 11

"Can't sleep?" Cole murmured in his ear, his arms tightening around Victor.

He sighed and opened his eyes, giving up on pretending like he was going to get any rest. His mate's bedroom was dark, except for the red numbers glowing on the nightstand that read 1:14. The house had been quiet for hours, Momma having gone to bed at her normal time and Ericka had been gone for weeks back to her dorm.

Turning in his mate's hold, he buried his face in the fragrant hollow of his throat and murmured, "No. Too nervous."

Cole didn't have to ask why, just rubbed Victor's back soothingly and held him as they lay together quietly. Finally, his deep voice broke the silence. "You know I'll still love you no matter what happens in the morning."

Tears pricked at Victor's eyes and his breath caught in his throat. He managed to croak out, "I thought we had an unspoken agreement?"

It had been a full month since he'd joined the pack and met his mate, but he and Cole hadn't said those words to each other yet. And they hadn't had sex or bitten each other. Victor knew that his mate had realized he was waiting to see what would happen with his wolf before telling him how he felt or finishing their mating. Even though they slept next to each other most nights and pleasured each other with their hands and mouths, Cole had accepted Victor's request to wait without question or hesitation.

Until now.

Victor wasn't sure what had changed except that they were scheduled to meet with Alpha Kincaid and Marcus in the morning so that Victor could try to shift for the first time since joining the pack. He'd tried not to be too optimistic, even though after about two weeks he'd been able to feel his wolf all the time, not just when he was emotional or around Rick.

"I decided that since it was unspoken, I wasn't actually bound to it." Victor could hear the smile in Cole's voice. "I know you think I'm going to change my mind if things don't work out how you hope tomorrow—"

"Not that you'd change your mind exactly—"

"But that's bullshit and I'm not going to pretend otherwise anymore."

Victor's breaths came quicker, fear and love fighting for dominance in his chest. He leaned back and peered up at his mate's tender face He was so scared. His heart knew— *knew*—that Cole's feelings for him wouldn't change, but it was like he couldn't convince his brain to accept that as truth. Or maybe it was his wolf, having been stunted and weakened for years. Maybe his wolf couldn't accept their mate's absolute adoration until after their meeting with Alpha Kincaid.

"You know I love you too, right?" he finally whispered, unable to hold the words back any longer now that Cole had said them.

"I do know that." Cole leaned forward and pressed a soft kiss to his mouth. "And I know nothing I say will be able to completely erase the fear you feel and that's okay too. I'll just keep showing you that we're forever, mate."

Victor squeezed his eyes shut but a tear slipped free. He wanted to apologize, to lie and tell Cole he wasn't afraid, to pretend he hadn't been damaged by his parents' treatment. But he didn't do any of that. He and Cole had talked things through so many times and Victor was finally getting to a place where he didn't automatically apologize for things that weren't his fault.

"I want to finish our mating, Victor," Cole said, his voice soft but firm. Victor's eyes popped open, but before he could say anything, Cole continued. "I know you were waiting to see about your shift, but... I think this will help."

"What do you mean?" he whispered, grabbing at Cole's bare skin and staring into his eyes.

"I mean... a part of you is worried this—us—is temporary and that I'll end up turning my back on you like your parents did. Like your old pack did."

Another tear slid down his face. "Cole, I..."

"Shhh, it's okay." Cole used his thumb to gently swipe at the tracks under Victor's eyes, then shifted on the bed until Victor was on his back and Cole was stretched out over him, surrounding him with his scent and his heat. "I just think... maybe your wolf and you would feel more secure in our mating if you had that irreversible connection. Something that would bind us together in a way even your wolf would understand."

Irreversible. Binding. Forever.

His wolf was howling in excitement at the idea of finally claiming his mate, and he knew his eyes were glowing because Cole's features were suddenly sharper. He supposed the answer about whether it was his wolf holding him back or not had been firmly decided. "I want to..."

"But?"

Victor stared into his mate's kind and patient eyes, then

slowly shook his head. What was he doing? He *loved* Cole, and Cole loved him. He knew it and he believed it and he wasn't going to let his doubts or his past come between them anymore. "No buts," he whispered. "I want to complete our mating."

Cole's yellow lion eyes suddenly shone in the room, and his deep purr vibrated against Victor's chest. "Are you sure?"

"I'm sure," he said without hesitation. Then Cole was kissing him, one of his big palms framing his face and holding him in place for Cole's drugging lips to devastate him. He moaned, louder than he probably should have, when Cole thrust his tongue into his mouth.

"Mm." Cole nibbled at his lips and then along his jaw to the side of his neck. "So sweet."

Victor giggled softly at the tickling sensation of his mate's teeth and stubble, but his laughter turned into a moan when Cole got to the juncture of his neck and shoulder and bit down harder. Goddess, he couldn't wait to wear his mate's bite with pride. "Cole."

"Yeah?"

Swallowing, he brought his hands up to cradle Cole's head as his mate kissed down his chest, stopping to lick at his nipples. "Don't tease me."

Cole's soft chuckle blew cool air across his hardened nub, causing his back to arch and toes to curl at the sensation. "Wasn't aware I was."

Gripping the sides of his mate's face, he pulled him back up and kissed him again, moaning when Cole got more aggressive and thrust his hardened cock against Victor's own. They were both only in their underwear, but that suddenly felt like ten layers of clothing. "We've had weeks of foreplay —don't make me wait," Victor muttered as he tried to tug down Cole's boxer briefs and also keep kissing him.

With a growl, Cole nipped at his bottom lip then surged up onto his knees, throwing the covers back to the end of the bed. Victor stared up at him, chest heaving, as the coolness of the room prickled at his exposed skin.

But the heat in Cole's eyes was warming certain parts of his body.

Cole reached down and snapped the elastic on the waistband of Victor's briefs and grinned fiercely when Victor gasped at the tiny sting. "You wanna top or bottom first?"

Goddess, that was a horribly unfair question. He wanted both, he wanted everything. When Cole raised a brow as he snuck the tips of his fingers under Victor's waistband and caressed the thin skin over his hip bones, Victor groaned. "Shit. Um. Bottom. I want to feel you inside me first."

"You remember what we talked about?" Cole asked, wasting no time in tugging off Victor's underwear and then wiggling out of his own. About a week before, Cole had explained to Victor that while he wouldn't have a knot when they mated, feline shifters had their own version. That his cock would swell and grow smooth ridges down his shaft...

To say Victor had been thinking about how it would feel would be an understatement.

"Definitely," he said, smirking and flipping around so he could reach the bedside table. He pulled the drawer out and found the lube. When he twisted around, holding the bottle out, he chuckled when he saw Cole's glowing gaze glued to his ass.

A month ago, he'd have blushed and stammered and turned over to hide himself. But after weeks of desperate touches and sweet words, Victor simply smiled, handed over the lube, and reveled in being on display for his mate. He pulled his knees up under him, planted his forearms on the mattress, and arched his spine.

"You know how sexy you look, don't you?" Cole said, dropping the bottle next to Victor's knee and grabbing ahold of Victor's ass with both hands.

Victor bit back a moan as Cole rubbed at his sensitive skin. "I know you think so, and that's all I care about."

Snorting, Cole didn't say anything else as he reached down and grabbed the discarded lube. Victor took a steadying breath and lowered his shoulders, relaxing as much as he could as he heard the lid click open behind him. When Cole's wet finger pressed against his hole, petting and circling the muscle, he shivered and tightened his grip on the sheets.

And waited.

And waited.

"Cole?"

"Hmm?"

"What're you doing back there?"

"Just enjoying the moment."

Huffing, Victor peered over his shoulder. "Seriously? I bet you could enjoy it a little more if you—" A high-pitched whine punched out of his chest cut him off as the result of Cole sinking an entire finger inside him. "Fucking... hell..."

"What was that you were saying?"

"Such a... jerk." He couldn't stop himself from moaning as Cole worked his finger in and out and chuckled. Victor lost the thread of conversation when he started working a second digit in next to the first. "Ah!"

"That's it," Cole murmured, using his free hand to rub up and down Victor's back. "Breathe and relax."

Sucking in a shuddery breath, Victor turned his head and pressed his cheek into the sheets, letting his eyes fall shut. The sensations radiating through his body were turning his bones to liquid and causing goosebumps to erupt down his arms.

Time slowed as Victor savored every flair of pleasure and stretching burn, the feelings becoming almost hypnotic. What could have been hours later, Cole slowly pulled his fingers free. A soft kiss was pressed to one of his cheeks, then Cole helped him flip over. He forced his eyes open as he stretched his limbs like he was waking from the best dream. His dick was so hard it ached, but only he could focus on was Cole spreading lubricant down his long cock. The head was large and the base of the shaft was thicker and Victor couldn't wait to feel it pushing inside him.

Cole smiled softly and stretched out over Victor, laying a slow, gentle kiss on his lax mouth. "Ready?" The way his lips brushed against Victor's when he spoke was intoxicating, and he made sure to stay close as he nodded, rubbing his tender lips against Cole's stubble and mouth.

Then Cole was pressing inside him and it was unlike anything Victor had ever felt before. Like being turned inside out and hit by lightning at the same time.

And he was addicted before Cole was even all the way in.

"Yes, yes, yes," he called, throwing his legs around Cole's waist and his arms around his shoulders.

Cole grunted as he thrust in the last inch, his heavy balls slapping against Victor's ass. For a long moment, they were frozen, panting against each other's necks, gripping at sweat-damp skin. When Cole's hips twitched, Victor gasped and tightened around him, drawing a groan from deep in his chest.

Pushing up, Cole stared down at him with glowing eyes and flushed cheeks, pulled his hips back, and thrust. Stars exploded behind Victor's eyes as he threw his head back and moaned. He never got the chance to catch his breath, Cole driving into him over and over, his searing gaze never leaving Victor's face.

Just as he saw the tips of Cole's fangs peeking out behind his upper lip, he felt his cock start to grow inside him. The swollen nodules massaging his inner walls and making his eyes roll back into his head.

"Look at me," Cole rasped out. When Victor peeled his eyes open, he sucked in a breath at the sight of Cole's fully extended fangs. Without thought or hesitation, Victor tipped his chin up and to the side, baring his neck. Hissing, Cole struck, one hand landing on Victor's hip and raising his ass off the mattress, driving in deep and releasing inside him.

The scent of Cole's come and the feel of his teeth in Victor's neck tightened the pooling desire in his gut, forcing his dick to erupt almost violently. Just as Cole released his teeth, Victor bared his own fangs and bit him.

A small, warm explosion in his chest surprised him into releasing Cole's skin. Their bond. He could really feel it. The connection between them that would always be there.

Forever.

Cole nuzzled at the side of his face. "Okay?"

"So okay," he said, panting and releasing his arms and legs so he was splayed on the mattress in a boneless heap. "I love you so much."

Swiping up his underwear, Cole paused to smile at him before using the cotton to wipe at their sticky skin. "I love you too."

"No matter what." It wasn't a question, but the way Cole's face softened into a tender expression let Victor know he heard the vulnerability.

"No matter what," Cole agreed, laid down next to him, and wrapped him in his big, strong arms.

As Victor settled, sleep finally coming for him, the warm presence of his mate deep in his chest next to his heart made him feel like he would be okay, no matter what happened in the morning.

CHAPTER 12

"You okay?" Cole couldn't take his eyes off his mate's fresh bonding bite mark, even though he knew Victor was anxious about trying to shift. Finishing their mating may have been a good idea to help Victor, but Cole had a feeling he and his lion would be easily distracted for a while. He vaguely remembered his dad telling him that when he gave him *the talk*.

Victor rubbed his palms on his thighs over and over, the soft sound of skin on jeans loud in the quiet Jeep. "Yeah, I'm fine."

Even if Cole couldn't see his nervous gestures or smell the sour hint of fear and anxiety in his scent, Cole would know his mate wasn't okay. The warm connection between them planted firmly in his chest was firing off tiny bolts of electricity instead of sitting passively in the background.

But he'd let him pretend. For now.

Reaching over, he clasped the back of Victor's neck, letting the heat of his skin soak into Victor's and smiling at the way his mate immediately relaxed under his touch.

Sighing, Victor laid a hand over his heart and threw a smile at Cole. "You were right about our mating. My wolf feels... settled, even though I'm worried. Being able to feel that connection is..."

Cole swept his thumb back and forth on the smooth skin behind Victor's ear. "Life changing."

Turning to stare at Cole with wide eyes, Victor nodded and whispered, "Exactly."

He glanced at the manor, knowing Alpha Kincaid would be waiting for them but not seeing any movement behind the bright winter sun reflecting off the windows. "Should we go in?"

Nodding, Victor unbuckled his seatbelt. "Yeah. I want to just get it over with. Sitting here freaking out won't change what's going to happen."

Instead of trying to reassure his mate for the thousandth time, Cole leaned in and kissed him softly, then turned the Jeep off and got out. Everyone who knew Victor could tell his wolf was stronger. At times, it seemed like the wolf's restless energy was vibrating out of Victor's skin, so Cole had a suspicion the shift would be a lot easier this time around for him. His wolf was more than ready to run free.

Hands clasped together, they hurried up to the front door, the brisk wind with the hint of snow in the air immediately making his eyes water. Fuck, he missed summer. He couldn't wait to lay out in the grass under the hot, oppressive sun in his shifted form.

Luckily, Marcus swung the large door open just before they reached it, ushering them in. His barely there smile seemed to dim when his eyes landed on Victor's mating bite scar as he peeled his winter coat off. Cole knew Marcus wasn't upset at their mating. Over the last month, he'd seen past the stoic mask enough times to realize Marcus truly cared about his cousin. But he knew that his time with Victor living with him was almost over.

"Ready?" Marcus asked, taking their coats from them and passing them off to a beta Cole didn't recognize.

Victor nodded, straightening his shoulders. "Yup."

Cole smiled indulgently behind his mate's back, so fucking proud of him. He trailed after the other two as Marcus led them through the massive house, Victor asking the occasional question as he twisted his head this way and that to see as much of the place as he could.

As they neared the back, a wonderful smell reached him. "Something smells good."

"The housekeeper, Mrs. Wilkins, is making breakfast for us to share afterward," Marcus said, pushing through a door into what turned out to be an enormous kitchen.

Cole spotted Alpha Kincaid right away, leaning back against a counter on the other side of the room, munching on an apple and smiling at the shorter woman bustling around him. Pushing off the marble, Kincaid murmured something to the housekeeper, then strolled toward them, his movements easy and full of untapped power.

"Morning," Alpha Kincaid greeted them, his normally deep voice extra gritty like he hadn't gotten much sleep. "You excited?"

Cole glanced at Victor, not surprised to find him biting nervously at his lower lip.

"Kind of. Kind of scared too," Victor said, honest as ever.

Kincaid's smile was kind as he gripped the side of Victor's neck, opposite of where his new bonding bite was. "Let's not make you wait around then, okay? It's just going to be the four of us. We'll step into the mudroom over there"—he tipped his head toward a door off the kitchen—"and then I'll give your wolf a little... push to help him come to the surface."

Victor sucked in a breath, his cheeks puffing out before he let it out in a rush. "Okay."

Alpha Kincaid chuckled. "It'll be easy. You'll see."

They all traipsed into the attached room that seemed half like a normal mudroom and half like a locker room. Kincaid nodded at the cubbies. "You can stash your clothes in one of those."

Taking one more steadying breath, Victor quickly stripped. Once he was naked, he turned and locked eyes with Alpha Kincaid. "I'm ready."

Kincaid stepped forward until he was only about a foot away from Victor. "Take two deep breaths and try and settle your heart rate a bit. Remember, you're safe here. This isn't like last time. There won't be any pain or fear." Victor's breaths and heart eventually slowed to match Alpha Kincaid's. "Good. You're doing really well, Victor. Keep breathing and close your eyes. See your wolf, feel his energy. He wants to come out, doesn't he?"

Victor's chin slowly moved up and down, but he didn't open his eyes. Kincaid's slow, easy cadence was almost hypnotizing it was so soothing.

"Keep picturing him," Kincaid murmured, taking one step backward. "Hold his shape in your mind. And relax. Good, Victor. You're going to feel a push from my magic. Don't fight it. Let it carry you through the shift. Ride it like a wave in the ocean."

The air around Victor shimmered for a moment, and then it happened. Victor's body began to bend and change, elongating and shrinking and sprouting fur. It was slower than Cole's shift, but the change was steady. The entire time, Alpha Kincaid kept murmuring what a good job Victor was doing. The atmosphere in the small room felt charged, like a storm was brewing in the center, Kincaid's magic licking at exposed skin and swelling larger and larger.

Finally, the magic began to ease and Victor was left standing on four paws in the middle of the room, dark brown and white fur beautiful in the winter light.

"You did it," Cole whispered, stumbling forward and dropping to his knees. Victor's whole body wiggled with excitement and he pushed into Cole's chest, licking at his face. "I knew you could. You did so good."

"Very well," Marcus said behind him.

Cole glanced back and grinned at him and Alpha Kincaid. Kincaid's eyes were shining fiercely, pride and affection evident in his face and scent. "Thank you."

He meant for everything: for letting Victor into the pack, caring for all of them, for helping his mate find joy in his wolf. Judging by Alpha Kincaid's smile, he understood. He threw an arm around Marcus's shoulders and tipped their heads together. Cole glanced away when Marcus's expression began to morph into something more in the safety of his alpha's embrace. It felt private, like something just between the alpha and his beta.

Rubbing at the soft fur on Victor's neck and ears, Cole grinned. "I suppose we should go for a run, huh?"

Barking, Victor practically spun in a circle.

"Okay, okay." He stood and pulled his shirt off in one motion, tossing it onto the pile of Victor's things. "We'd be honored if you joined us, Alpha Kincaid."

"Easy, pup," Kincaid said, laughing, as Victor jumped onto his legs, tongue hanging out. "I have time for a quick one."

"I should—" Marcus started to say, but their alpha's snort stopped him short.

"If I'm going, so are you. Get naked, Marcus."

Cole laughed as he finished stripping, but paused before shifting, eyeing the door that led outside. His lion was big and he wasn't sure if he'd fit through the space. Grimacing, he realized he'd have to step outside in the snow with his bare feet.

"Come on, mate," he called as he tugged the door open and immediately shivered. "Ah shit."

Laughter behind him made him want to flip the bird, but he didn't think his alpha would appreciate that. Bracing himself, he darted out into the four-inch-deep snow and hissed. As soon as he was clear of the doorway though, he began to shift. Within five strides, he was on fours, shaking out his large mane and growling.

"Whoa."

He turned to find his alpha standing just inside the mudroom in his underwear, eyes locked on Cole's lion.

"Damn. Marcus, remind me to ask Cole about being a beta over breakfast."

Cole snorted and shook his head, annoyed that he couldn't tell him about Ericka but reluctant to shift back to have the conversation while he stood in the snow, naked.

Victor darted out around Kincaid's legs, hopping around in the snow like a puppy. Appearing behind Rick's shoulder, Marcus's thin pale body immediately began to flush from the cold.

"He doesn't want to be a beta, but his sister does. Ericka?" The way Marcus said her name made Cole think it wasn't the first time he'd mentioned her to Kincaid. Sure enough, the alpha nodded.

"That's right. You and Bennett mentioned that." Kincaid looked at Cole thoughtfully, like he was imagining a lioness in his place. "You know, they say the females are much tougher anyway."

Cole roared, unable to stop himself from protesting the implication he was weak in front of his mate. Kincaid's eyes flared bright but he just laughed.

"Easy, Cole." He stepped back into the room, then reappeared a moment later without his last piece of clothing. From one breath to the next, he shifted into an enormous black wolf. Cole was stunned. He'd never seen anyone shift so fast before.

Victor, who'd run off to sniff at a hundred different things, came running back, yipping excitedly at their alpha's wolf. Compared to the size of Kincaid, Victor really did look like a pup. And even when Marcus came out, shut the door, and shifted, he was bigger than Victor's wolf too.

When Kincaid playfully snapped his teeth, sending Victor tumbling back into the snow, joy filled Cole. He'd run and played with his family plenty as his lion, but having his alpha there, chasing after Victor as he went running toward the trees, was a gift in and of itself.

As powerful and aggressive and stern as Rick Kincaid could be, this side of him was just as valuable in his ability to be an alpha in Cole's opinion. To share in the simple pleasure of running through the woods, chasing packmates and squirrels, showed his real strength of character.

An hour later, the four of them were stuffed into the booth in the manor's kitchen, devouring everything the housekeeper put in front of them. Victor was snuggled up against Cole, a little loopy from the experience of running with pack for the first time.

"Your lion is so pretty," he whispered loudly, smacking a syrupy kiss on Cole's cheek.

"Thank you," he said, grinning despite the snickers coming from the other side of the table. He didn't think he'd ever felt happier or more at ease in whole life. He had his family, their diner, his mate, and an alpha who took care of them in every way they needed.

"Can I braid your mane sometime?"

EPILOGUE

About three years later...

"*I* appreciate you doing this," Bennett said, his voice lowered even though the other man with them was human and on the other side of Cole's ramshackle house, surveying the property.

Cole waved a hand and leaned back against the front of his Jeep, folding his arms over his chest. "Don't worry about it. After everything you've done for me and my family, the least I can do is let some random guy check out the property I've been looking to sell for years."

"To the *right* person. You've turned down a lot of offers over the years—some of which came from people I sent your way." B grimaced and matched his stance, his large muscles bulging under his T-shirt. "This is probably a terrible idea. He's—"

"After what he did for your mate? For this pack?" Cole scoffed and gave the pack second a hard look. "Stop acting like I'm doing you this huge favor. Though... I haven't agreed to sell it, technically."

Bennett backpedaled fast. "Oh, no, I know that. And he

knows that too." He jerked his head toward where the guy was now standing with his back to them and the house, hands on his hips, staring at the woods behind the property. "And there's no pressure—"

"Man, I'm messing with you." Cole stepped away from his vehicle, slowly lowering his arms and running his eyes carefully over the Enforcer. "Are you okay? You're not so easily... riled usually."

Running a hand over his bare head, B squeezed the back of his neck and looked away from Cole. "You know, I think I liked it better when you were intimidated by me."

That made Cole laugh loud enough the blond guy looked over at them, but he turned back to the trees almost immediately. "No, you didn't. And after all the meals and conversations we've shared over the years, I think you know you can trust me." Getting serious, he captured and held B's dark eyes. "What's going on?"

Bennett pressed his lips together and shook his head, which told Cole all he needed to know without the other man having to say a word. The only things B was close-mouthed about were high-level pack stuff. Cole nodded and stepped back, his eyes finding the human moving toward them slowly through the over-grown grass.

"Things are going to get worse before they get better, aren't they?" he murmured, keeping his eyes on the guy as he got closer.

Bennett glanced at the other man too, but the deep lines in his forehead and around his mouth spoke volumes. "Probably," he said, his voice barely loud enough for even Cole's ears to catch. "And I'm worried about who else we'll end up in bed with before the end..."

They let the conversation drop as the blond man came up next to them and grinned. "How much?"

Bennett sighed. "I told you Cole may not be interested in selling it to you."

He couldn't help but chuckle as the human rolled his eyes. "It's okay, B," Cole said, then pulled his phone out of his pocket when it vibrated. He smiled at the message from Victor. Tucking it back into his jeans, he gave the guy a onceover. "Are you really what they say you are?"

The blond's smile was more than a little predatory, even for a human. "That matter?"

"Maybe."

Dark green eyes narrowed, then the man looked away and shrugged nonchalantly, a small braid with purple beads catching the sun when his long hair flared with the movement. When he met Cole's gaze again, there was a hardness behind his eyes that hadn't been there before. "Yeah. Yeah, I am."

Cole glanced at Bennett, but his usually open face was locked down, giving nothing away and leaving the decision completely up to Cole. But he'd known what he was going to do as soon as he'd gotten B's call. For the first time, the idea of selling the property he'd bought on a whim hadn't left him feeling queasy.

He held out his hand. "I think we can come to some sort of arrangement."

After hashing out preliminary details with Bennett and the human, Cole stopped at the diner for a couple hours to catch up on paperwork, but they'd had to hire so much help over the last few years he wasn't needed there as much. He still ran the backend of things and picked up shifts in the dining room when needed, but he didn't have to work seven days a week to keep them afloat anymore.

After he finished inputting invoices and getting payroll situated, he headed home, and he still beat Victor somehow. Now that he was finally selling the property outside of town, he realized he and Victor could get their own place. The idea of not having his sister and mom around all the time didn't fill him with relief like he thought. The four of them had formed a solid, dependable unit that he was reluctant to break up. Though he doubted Ericka would stay forever. She was busy at the manor most days with her duties as a pack beta, but at some point, she'd want her own space or maybe she'd meet her mate and they'd get a place together.

He was just stepping into his and Victor's bedroom, towel wrapped around his waist and skin still damp, when Victor bounded in with a wildness in his movements and excitement in his scent that always followed a run in his shifted form.

"Have fun?" Cole asked, settling on the end of their bed, towel parting up his thigh as he leaned back on his hands. He did his best to hide his grin at the feral look in Victor's eyes as he stared at all of Cole's exposed skin.

"Yeah," he said absently, gaze fixating on a drop of water Cole could feel running down his chest. "Ericka and I went swimming in the creek behind the manor with a couple of other betas, then her and I just ran for a bit."

"You stayed inside—"

Victor's face softened a little, and he refocused on Cole's eyes. "Yes. We stayed well-within the wards."

As safe as Cole felt in their pack, the fact remained that things had changed in the last few months. Something was coming, targeting their pack for some reason, and Cole worried when Victor was out of his sight. Luckily, they'd gained a few more powerful witches over the years and were able to protect themselves more than other packs could. But he'd take his cues from Bennett and Marcus and the others— and right now, they were worried. They were holed up in the manor more often than they used to be, barely visiting the diner or other pack establishments.

"How'd it go at the house?" Victor asked, pulling his shirt off and completely derailing Cole's wayward thoughts.

His mate was so hot. He'd put on a little weight over the years thanks to eating well and running as his wolf regularly. He'd always be more slender than Cole, but he'd added muscle and filled out in his arms and chest and legs. And added a little more curve to his ass.

Victor popped the button on his jeans but left them on and crawled onto Cole's lap, straddling him. "Is he really a… you know?"

Cole chuckled as he sat up and wrapped his arms around his waist. "He is and… I'm going to sell it to him anyway."

Victor jerked his head up from where he'd started nuzzling at Cole's bonding scar. "You are? Really?"

Nodding, he stared into Victor's honey brown eyes, savoring the warmth of their bond like it was brand new and not years old. There was no judgement on Victor's face, no fear in his scent. He trusted that Cole had done the right thing for them as mates and for the pack. "Yeah, really. It just felt like it was time. There was something about him that felt like he was who I'd been waiting for." He grimaced. "I know it doesn't make sense—"

"Doesn't have to make sense to me," Victor said, voice fierce. "You've taken care of me and your family for years, always doing right by us. I trust you and your instincts."

Cole swallowed, trying to dislodge the lump in his throat, and ran his hands up Victor's bare back. "You know what this means, right?"

"We'll finally be able to replace that piece of crap stove downstairs with some of the money from the sale?"

Cole laughed, though it quickly turned to a groan when Victor leaned in and nipped at his bonding scar. "I was thinking more along the lines of getting our own place."

There was no reply for a long moment as Victor used his teeth, tongue, and lips on his neck and throat, driving Cole crazy. Finally, his mated grunted his frustration at not being able to reach more of Cole's skin. He smiled as Victor prodded him farther back onto the bed, familiar with how his mate was after a run, his wolf still close to the surface. The only way he could describe it was Victor liked to *aggressively* cuddle.

Once he was settled firmly on his back, towel tossed to the floor and Victor pressed all down his front with his arms and legs wrapped around him, he tried to pick up the conversation again. "Are you still firmly against living outside of town?"

Victor huffed a laugh, his warm breath washing over the thin skin of Cole's throat and making him shiver. "I could maybe be convinced."

Smiling up at the ceiling, Cole tucked one of his hands behind his head. He really was one of the luckiest people in the world. His mate had walked into his life when he'd least expected it, but ever since they'd met, Cole felt like he was basking in the summer sun year-round.

"I don't want to leave Momma and Ericka yet though," Victor said after long minutes of peaceful silence, rubbing his face into Cole throat. "Not while things are so unsettled with the pack."

"Agreed. Which gives us plenty of time to find the perfect place."

Victor pressed a kiss into his scar. "And maybe when we find our new house, we can ask Ericka about..."

"Being our surrogate?" he finished, excitement building in his belly just at the words. He hadn't told Victor but he'd already casually mentioned it to his sister and she'd been on board immediately.

Victor squirmed against him and whispered, "Yeah."

Closing his eyes, Cole pictured a tiny little girl with Ericka's curls and Victor's warm brown eyes. He and Victor would be fantastic dads—he was sure of it.

"Your scent just got really strong," Victor murmured, inhaling audibly.

"I'm really happy. I love you so much and can't wait to start our family."

Victor scoffed. "We already are a family."

"You're right." He pressed a kiss into Victor's soft curls. "Well, I can't wait to expand it."

"Me either." Victor released a soft breath, his muscles relaxing as his heart rate slowed. "I'm so glad I came in for that job interview."

"Me too, mate." He inhaled Victor's sourdough scent and let himself imagine a thousand more moments just like this one. And a couple cubs running underfoot. And his mom smothering all of them with love.

He couldn't wait to see what the future would bring.

Thank you for reading Cole & Victor's story! I hope you enjoyed getting to know the Kincaid Pack.

You can continue the pack's journey in the first book of the series, The Alpha and His King, *where grumpy, workaholic Rick meets his match in sweet and caring Kai.*

NEXT IN SERIES!

When Kai flies out of a shed, swinging a rake, Rick's life flips upside down.

As alpha, Rick's dedication to his pack has never wavered —until Kai. The pull he feels toward the younger man is more than a simple distraction, but Rick won't let himself lose focus. Not while a hidden enemy is drawing near.

Moving in with the grumpy alpha who saved him is a big change for Kai, and it isn't long before he begins to ache for something he can't have. As a half-human shifter responsible for his three younger siblings, he knows he can never be Rick's mate.

Pushing aside their doubts and insecurities, they grow closer. But when the pack's enemies strike, bringing their fears to fruition, Rick and Kai have to decide if they're willing to risk it all to be together.

The Alpha and His King *is the first book in the Kincaid Pack series and features a quick-tempered and possessive alpha; a sweet and feisty alpha-mate; shifters, seers, and witches galore; massive amounts of hurt/comfort; and a happily ever after.*

Available in ebook, paperback, audiobook, and KU!

ALSO BY KIKI CLARK

Kincaid Pack Series
The Alpha and His King (Rick & Kai)
The Second and His Bonded (Kieran & Bennett)
The Deputy and His Enforcer (Marcus & Robson)
The Hunter and His Mates (Gabriel & Jamie & Drake)
The Enforcer and His Heart (Nico & Keegan)
The Witch and His Doctor (Carter & Damien)

Kincaid Pack Adult Coloring Book

Kincaid Pack Universe Standalone
The Mobster's Mate (Quinten & Caden)

Trident Agency Series (written with EM Lindsey)
Sunshine (Remi & Jeremiah)
Priest (Oliver & Priest)

Blue Collar Hearts Series
Out In the Cold (Beau & Coop)
Laying Pipe (John & Lukas)
Banger (Hank & Kevin)

Leather & Chrome Series

Reckless (Tank & CJ)

Temptation (Six & Ollie)

Yearning (Houston & Kenneth)

Joyful (Rooster & Emmett)

Possession (Tomas & Mason & Vinnie)

Forever Family Trilogy

Favor (Declan & Jeremy)

Easy (Simon & Jackson)

Faker (Will & Samuel)

Trilogy Boxset — *Best deal!*

Many of my books are also available in audio! Be sure to check out my website or Audible.com.

ABOUT THE AUTHOR

A small-town Michigan girl, Kiki has enjoyed reading since she first picked up a YA fantasy as a child. After that, she devoured everything she could get her hands on and dreamed of one day writing her own books that touched people's hearts.

In 2020, she proudly joined the ranks of authors releasing character-driven, emotionally satisfying books showcasing that everyone deserves to find love.

To keep up-to-date with Kiki, sign up for her newsletter: http://www.kikiclark.com/newsletter.

Keep in touch by following her on any of these platforms:

facebook.com/kikiclarkauthor

instagram.com/kikiclark2017

amazon.com/author/kikiclark

bookbub.com/authors/kiki-clark

goodreads.com/kikiclark

www.ingramcontent.com/pod-product-compliance
Lightning Source LLC
Chambersburg PA
CBHW060234180626
46813CB00007B/3074